The End of the World *is Los Angeles*

The End of the World

AWP-4

is Los *Angeles*

Stories by François Camoin

University of Missouri Press
Columbia and London, 1982

Copyright © 1982 by François Camoin
University of Missouri Press, Columbia, Missouri 65211
Library of Congress Catalog Card Number 81–16166
Printed and bound in the United States of America

Library of Congress Cataloging in Publication Data

Camoin, François André, 1939–
    The end of the world is los angeles, and other stories.

    "AWP–4."
    Contents: Lieberman's father—Things I did to make it
possible—Teller, the bear and the yellow thunderbird—[etc.]
    I. Title
PS3553.A437L5   813′.54   81–16166
ISBN 0–8262–0365–5   AACR2

Some of the stories in this collection have appeared
or are forthcoming in the following magazines:

"Teller, the Bear and the Yellow Thunderbird,"
        Vanderbilt Review (Texas).
"Superman," *Western Humanities Review.*
"The Vanishing," *Cimarron Review.*
"My Life Is a Screenplay," *California Quarterly.*
"Now She Sleeps," *Chelsea Magazine.*
"Lieberman's Father," *Missouri Review.*
"A Grown Man," *Utah Holiday.*

This one is for Nancy and for Shane

With special thanks to Albin Krietz

Contents

Lieberman's Father, 1

Things I Did to
    Make It Possible, 15

Teller, the Bear and
    the Yellow Thunderbird, 19

Drowning in California, 28

Superman (Georgia's Dream), 40

The Vanishing, 47

A Grown Man, 56

A Marriage, 62

Now She Sleeps, 71

My Life Is a Screenplay, 85

The End of the World *is Los Angeles*

Lieberman's Father

Lieberman had his eyes on his chicken salad and so at first didn't see the woman. She stopped short at his table and stood, swaying a little this way and that, looking like a person who has just bumped into something and is wondering if she's hurt herself. To the people at the next table it was clear that what she'd bumped into was Lieberman.

"Excuse me," she said.

Lieberman looked up. He saw a thin woman who looked athletic, like a jogger, well-preserved. He thought she might be fifty years old, might be sixty.

"Hello, Martin."

"Do I know you?" Lieberman said.

"No," she told him. She pulled out a chair and sat down across the table from him. "A little water? You don't mind? It's a shock."

Lieberman poured for her. "What's a shock?"

"This isn't going to be easy for you."

Lieberman laid down his fork. "What isn't?"

She emptied her glass and set it back on the table. "That's better." She sat back and looked Lieberman in the eye. Her face was attractive, he thought. Serious.

"I'm your father," she said.

Lieberman looked around. If anybody had heard the woman they didn't make a sign. No heads turned.

"Did I understand you?" Lieberman said.

"I'm your real father," the woman said.

"I have a father. He's sixty-eight years old and lives in New Jersey. He's a retired carpenter."

"I know," she said. "A religious man. He never had much time for his family." She coughed. "Would you mind if I had a little more water?" She drank it slowly, looking over the rim of the glass at Lieberman.

"You followed me in here," he said.

"To tell the truth, yes. Don't get mad. This is the first time I've seen you up close like this in fifteen years. This California weather doesn't agree with me. Not enough humidity—a person could dry out like a dead leaf if he doesn't drink water all the time." She studied Lieberman. "You don't look bad. A little heavy, maybe. But you have a good tan, good muscle tone. I can see you take care of yourself."

"What's it all about?" Lieberman said. "What do you want from me?"

"Forty-six years old. And you have your own discount store already: eighteen departments, though I understand cameras aren't doing so well. But at your age that's something. You should be proud."

"I have a partner," Lieberman said.

"Segal? I've seen Segal. Don't worry, I didn't tell him who I am—I don't want to cause you embarrassment. Segal's a money man; it's your ideas that make the place go, am I right?"

Lieberman felt himself blush. "Maybe."

"You've done all right. Two daughters, Ruth at UCLA and Laura married to a psychologist. And you have a beautiful wife, even if she is a *shikse.*"

"She converted," Lieberman said.

The woman shrugged. "To Reformed. What kind of a Jew is that? Might as well be a Unitarian."

"Excuse me," Lieberman said, "but what business is this of yours? Why am I discussing my family with somebody who followed me into a restaurant?"

"They're my family too," the woman said.

"Enough is enough," Lieberman said. He signaled to the waitress for his check.

"Don't believe me—it's still God's truth. I'm your real father, Martin."

He left money on the table and walked away. When he was outside he looked back through the plate-glass window. She was still at his table. She poured herself another glass of water, looked up, waved at Lieberman.

Sheila Lieberman liked to eat dinner out on the patio under the trees, where she could look out over the Valley. "What's the sense of living in California if you can't eat outside?" she said when Lieberman complained about the heat and the smog.

"Maybe it was Segal," she said. "He has a peculiar idea of a joke sometimes. He could have hired this woman to do it so he could see your face tomorrow morning."

Lieberman shook his head. "Segal's idea of a joke is a rubber fly under my napkin at lunch. He wouldn't spend that kind of money for a laugh."

"Then it was a crazy person."

"What else?"

"I don't know. Maybe you ought to call your father and ask him."

"Ask him what?" Lieberman said. "If he's really my father? He's sixty-eight years old; he's doing what he always wanted to do all his life; he locks himself up with his books all day and he's happy as a clam. I'm going to ask him now, after forty-six years, if he's really my father? Long-distance?"

A gust of wind brought down a shower of dry brown needles and Lieberman covered his plate with his hands. He saw that the disease was spreading. On his last visit the tree-surgeon had folded Lieberman's check into his pocket without thanks. "We'll give it a little time. See how it responds. But I think you'll have to cut it down."

"It's dying," Sheila said, following Lieberman's look.

"We'll see." He began to eat slowly. "What would I tell him?" he said. "My father and I haven't talked in twenty years except to say hello and how are you once a month on the telephone. He doesn't want to talk to me."

"You love him," Sheila said.

"He doesn't know what love is," Lieberman said.

The next day he looked closely at Segal to see if the other man was playing a joke after all. They shared one big office at the store, with desks that faced each other on opposite sides of the room. They also shared Miss Lash, a graduate of the Bryman School who could type like a machine-gun and take dictation faster than the partners could talk. Lieberman suspected that Segal was taking her out at night, but in the office she treated them both with the same impersonal courtesy.

"I talked to my father on the phone yesterday," Lieberman said.

Segal looked up from the invoices and order blanks scattered on his desk. "He's still in New Jersey?" Lieberman saw nothing out of the ordinary in his partner's face. "You ought to tell him to come settle out here—it's healthier. Lots of nice places down by Laguna Beach; he could be with people his own age."

"You know how it is," Lieberman said. "He doesn't want to take a chance. What if he didn't like it?"

The store stayed open every night until ten o'clock, but except at inventory time or when there was trouble with one of the departments Lieberman was gone by six. Home was a slow twenty-minute drive along Ventura Boulevard; it gave him time to put the store out of his mind and become a family man again. Lieberman didn't want to be like his father, who had come home five days a week, put away his carpenter's tools and disappeared into the little room he'd added to the back of the house, where he kept his books. On Saturdays he'd been gone all day, of course, and on Sundays it was the books again. Lieberman wanted a different kind of life. Also he felt that Sheila needed him. Now that both the girls were gone from the house she had become moody: sometimes sad, sometimes unnaturally gay. Sometimes she sat close to Lieberman on the couch, not satisfied unless some part of herself was touching him; other nights she disappeared into her sewing-room and watched her twelve-inch TV until Lieberman gave up and went to bed.

This night she chose television, and Lieberman lay in the bedroom for a long time, staring up into the dark, only half in control of the thoughts that flew through his head. When he finally fell asleep it was to dream of the woman sho said she was his father. In the dream she lived in the old family house in New Jersey and she kept calling Lieberman long-distance in California. "Come home, Martin. It's healthier out here; you could be with your own kind of people."

A week went by and Lieberman stopped expecting to see the woman again. Los Angeles is full of crazy people—what's one more? He thought about Segal and Miss Lash: were they going out nights together? What could he do about it? Then he came out of the store a few minutes late, opened the front door of his Buick, and found her sitting in the passenger seat reading a paperback novel, waiting for him. She bent down the corner of a page to mark her place.

"Did you call your father and ask him?" she said.

"I call him every month," Lieberman said. "What should I ask?"

"Your mother was nineteen years old when she married him," the woman said. Seeing her close up in the light from the parking-lot lamps, Lieberman realized she must have been quite handsome when she was young. Her voice was a strong contralto; like her face it had character.

"Look," he said, "I don't know who you really are . . ."

"Your father was away all day long; sometimes when he was working a job out of town he didn't get home until after dark. Your mother was lonely—it was her first time away from her family. What happened was the most natural thing in the world. She shouldn't be blamed."

"My mother died fifteen years ago," Lieberman said harshly.

"I was at the funeral. I don't suppose you remember."

"No," Lieberman said. He unlocked the ignition and started the motor. "I've had a long day; I want to go home."

"I was the same age as your mother," the woman said. "I was in college studying mathematics."

"At Princeton?"

"Columbia. I was home for the summer."

Lieberman pushed impatiently at the accelerator; the car roared and rocked slightly without moving forward. The transmission was still in Park.

"I was in my last year already," the woman said. "I started college at sixteen."

"A genius," Lieberman said sarcastically.

"I told you," the woman said. "You're a success because you come from good stock. Not that some of it isn't due to your own efforts, naturally."

"Enough!" Lieberman shouted.

"Go on, get angry, it'll do you good."

"How could anybody believe this?"

"Let it out. Yell if you want to."

"Get out of my car," Lieberman said. He reached across her and opened the far door; when she was outside he yanked the door shut. She stood there while he drove away. When he looked in the mirror she hadn't moved.

He drove slowly along Ventura Boulevard, past Coldwater and Woodman, not hearing the music on the radio. On the corner of Van Nuys there was a bar and he slowed down, but as he was turning into the parking lot he thought he saw Segal with his arm around Miss Lash going in the front door; he drove on.

"You're late," Sheila said. The television was off; she was listening to a record.

Lieberman let himself sink slowly into a chair. "She was there again," he said. "I don't want to talk about it."

"So don't talk about it. She's a crazy person—tell her to leave you alone."

"I did."

"She won't."

"I know," Lieberman said.

"I had a call from Laura today."

"Good. How is she?"

"Not good."

"What did she say?"

"Nothing. We just chatted. But I could tell by her voice."

"She didn't tell you anything?"

"No."

"Well then we'll have to wait until she does. I never did want her to marry David Shupack," Lieberman said. "Even if he is a psychologist. He doesn't have feelings."

"Everybody has feelings," Sheila said.

Lieberman shrugged. "As long as she loves him."

The record ended and Sheila got up to turn it over. "I looked at the tree again today," she said. "It's getting worse."

"Maybe it needs more water."

"It's already like a swamp around the roots."

"Maybe we're watering it too much," Lieberman said. "Call the man tomorrow and have him come over and take a look."

"Every time he comes it's twenty dollars and all he has is bad news."

"I love that tree," Lieberman said. "I don't have time to plant another one and wait ten years for it to grow to where we can enjoy it. Call. What's twenty dollars?"

He pressed his face against the window; in the patio floodlights the pine looked healthy but Lieberman knew his wife and the tree-surgeon were right—it was dying.

"I'll cut it down myself," he said.

The next morning he went to the hardware department and picked out a chainsaw and two coils of nylon rope. He set them by his desk and Segal looked at him curiously, but he didn't explain. Did Miss Lash look tired under the makeup? He couldn't be sure. Segal had bags under his eyes, but Segal always had bags under his eyes. Was it any of his business? He put it out of his mind and made plans to straighten out the camera department.

At noon he rolled his chair back and stretched. Segal was dictating a letter; Miss Lash was keeping up without effort.

"Lunch?" Lieberman said.

Segal shook his head. "I'm not really hungry. You go ahead; maybe I'll send out for a sandwich later."

The delicatessen on Sepulveda was full of real-estate salesmen talking loudly and Lieberman stopped in the doorway, undecided. Sometimes David Shupack took time from his mental-health clinic to eat here, but Lieberman didn't see him. What could he have said to his son-in-law anyhow? What's the matter between you and Laura? I know there's trouble because Sheila heard it in her voice the last time she called? Cahn was sitting at a back table with some of his friends; he waved at Lieberman to come over. Why did he shave, Lieberman thought; he looks terrible without a beard. And the cowboy clothes—everybody wants to look like something he's not. Lieberman had heard something about Cahn and his wife; if he went over there Cahn would probably tell him about it, and he didn't want to know. He waved back; the waitress was coming his way with a sheaf of menus but he shook his head at her and went back out to his car. Maybe he'd have a sandwich with Segal.

But when he got back the office door was locked. He tried his key; the cylinder turned and the bolt slid back but the door didn't give. Lieberman put his ear to the wooden panel and heard scurrying inside, and low urgent voices. Segal and Miss Lash. He turned and walked out; as he passed the perfume counter the girls giggled.

Sheila was surprised to see him. "You never come home for lunch on Wednesday. Is something wrong at the store? You want to eat?"

"Fix me anything," Lieberman said. "Chicken salad, an egg, anything."

He ate without hunger, to fill his stomach. Sheila perched on a kitchen stool and watched him. "Can you believe it?" Lieberman said. He pushed the plate to one side. "Right in the office during lunch time. The door wouldn't open, thank God. I think he had the good sense to put a chair under the knob otherwise I would have walked right in on them."

"It's the time of life," Sheila said. "A man his age—you could almost expect it."

"What age?" Lieberman said. "Segal's forty-six. My age. A year older than you."

"I looked out the window this morning," Sheila said, "and I think I saw that woman. The one who's been following you."

Lieberman's heart gave a jump. "Are you sure?"

"How could I be sure? I've never seen her before. But there was a woman hanging around across the street looking at this house. She looked like a nice person. Not crazy."

"What did you do?"

"I couldn't decide. What if it was just someone out for a walk? So I went out to talk to her, but she was gone."

"She'll be back," Lieberman said. "If she comes to the door don't answer. I don't want you to get mixed up in this if she's crazy."

"If?" Sheila said.

"You know what I mean. Maybe I'll call David tonight and ask him what he thinks."

"He's a marriage counselor. What would he know about crazy women?"

"A psychologist is a psychologist. He went to seven years of school; they must have taught him something besides marriage problems."

"Don't talk to him about Laura."

"All right," Lieberman promised.

"And don't be too hard on Segal. It might happen to you someday."

"Not with the secretary."

"Don't be so sure," Sheila told him. "People get desperate."

When Lieberman opened the office door he saw that Miss Lash was gone.

"I gave her the afternoon off," Segal said.

"How long have we been partners?" Lieberman said.

"I don't know. Eight years?"

"Nine."

"Are you going to give me a lecture on not fooling around with the help? Don't you think I know already?"

Lieberman searched for words. "In the office?" he said. "With everybody out there? They knew what you were doing. It isn't civilized."

Segal hung his head. "All of a sudden she was so beautiful. Little tits like oranges. I could see them under her blouse. It made me crazy. You were supposed to be gone to lunch."

"At least thank God for the chair under the doorknob," Lieberman said.

"That was her idea. I couldn't think—I was like a madman. She likes me, Lieberman. We have good times together. We even talk."

The great pleasure in his eyes made Lieberman feel defeated. "We can't keep her," he said.

"You're right," Segal said. "I'll find her another job."

"All right." He got up and slapped Segal on the back, awkwardly. "All the same," he said, "you're being a damn fool."

"I know," Segal said. Lieberman heard him mutter to himself, "But it's so fine."

When Lieberman talked to his son-in-law on the telephone he was never quite certain that he wasn't actually talking to somebody else. David Shupack had a completely neutral voice. Lieberman explained about the woman.

"Cases like this aren't exactly run-of-the-mill," David said. "But they're not unheard of."

"She knows everything about me," Lieberman said.

"People who are crazy in one way often function very well in other ways. Knowing all about you helps her convince herself of her fantasy, so she does some research. It's all part of the pattern."

"I thought you psychologists never used that word *crazy.*"

"Maladjusted, neurotic—what's a word? She's not in touch."

"This is your opinion? She's nuts?"

"Without meeting her myself I can't tell for sure, naturally."

"What else could it be?"

"The *world* is a crazy place," David said. "Who knows, really?" There was something odd happening to his voice.

"How's Laura?" Lieberman said. Sheila hissed a warning; he waved it away. "How's my little girl?" he said.

A strange sound came back to Lieberman through the telephone. "What's that?" he said. "Are you there, David?" The sound stopped and Lieberman realized that his son-in-law had been crying. "David?"

The neutral voice, when it came back, had an odd dignity that Lieberman didn't remember having heard in it before. "Martin, I think she's seeing another man. She's leaving me, Martin."

"The whole fucking world is falling apart," Lieberman said to his wife when he hung up the phone.

"You never swear," she said.

"I wouldn't be surprised if she *is* seeing somebody else," he said.

"David wouldn't be the first husband who's imagining things. Who really knows?"

"He's a cold fish," Lieberman said. "Who could blame her?"

"I'm going to watch a little TV," Sheila said. "Don't wait up for me."

"Good night," Lieberman said.

He began to look for the crazy woman and caught himself feeling disappointed because he didn't see her. She didn't come to the house again, and she didn't come to the store. She's crazy, of course, Lieberman told himself, but that doesn't mean she might not have some good advice for me. People who are crazy in one way often function very well in other ways. If she was going to disappear like that why did she come into my life at all? Once he thought he saw her going down the aisle between calculators and infant wear, but when he tapped her on the shoulder she turned out to be just another old woman with an unpleasant face. A California face.

He called his father in New Jersey but from the first hello Lieberman could tell that the old man didn't want to talk to him about anything that mattered.

"Were you in the middle of something important?" he said.

"What's important?" Lieberman could see his father, three thousand miles away, shrugging his shoulders.

"I didn't want to interrupt anything, that's all. Do you want me to call you back later?"

"No, no. Talk. How are you? How's the family?"

"Fine," Lieberman said bitterly.

"You don't sound good."

Lieberman had intended to be calm, but his good intentions evaporated. "It's everything," he said. "Sheila's going through some crazy thing, watching television every night until three in the morning; Laura's having trouble in her marriage; my partner's running around with a twenty-year-old girl and says he can talk to her. Talk!"

"Stop," his father said.

"What?"

"Martin, I'm old. I'm sorry you're having trouble in your life, but to tell the truth I don't want to hear about it. Don't tell me details."

"My tree's dying," Lieberman said.

"What tree? What's that about a tree? Are you crazy?"

"It's dying," Lieberman said. He hung up.

He sat with his head in his hands. From the sewing room he could hear the sound of a television quiz show.

The telephone rang. "You hung up on your father?"

"I'm sorry," Lieberman said.

"It's nothing personal," his father said. "For more than sixty years I've had troubles of my own and now I want to be done with it. I have a right to a little peace. Call me any time, but don't tell me everything. Just in general."

"In general I'm going crazy," Lieberman said.

"Everything'll work out in time," his father said. "Try not to get worked up so much. Sheila's a good girl—I always liked her."

"So why didn't you come to the wedding?" Lieberman said.

"That's all past. Why bring it up now after twenty years?"

"Just once," Lieberman said, "couldn't you tell me you made a mistake, you're sorry?"

"What good would that do?"

"I don't know," Lieberman said. "I'd like to hear it, that's all."

"Forget it," his father said. "That's my advice. Don't be so concerned with wrongs done to you. Past is past. Call me again when you feel better. In the meantime take care of yourself."

In the morning Lieberman stepped out in his robe to pick up the *L. A. Times* and saw the woman standing at the corner, half-hidden behind a flowering bush. He waved the folded newspaper. "Hey!" he called out. "Wait a minute."

He thought she smiled at him, but he was too far away to be certain. "Wait!" he shouted. But she was already gone.

"You should be glad she didn't insist on talking to you again," Sheila told him. "Maybe this means she's giving up her craziness and she's going to leave you alone."

"There was something very nice about her," Lieberman said. "I could tell she was a warm person even if she was crazy."

The rest of the story? You know it already. You know Lieberman: he's like you and me. How else could it happen?

Lieberman stands at the bottom of the tree with the saw throbbing in his hand, preparing himself for the first cut. "Are you sure you know what you're doing?" Sheila says.

"First the front notch, then the back cut," Lieberman recites. He's been reading a book from the public library. "It has to fall right there." The psychiatrist next door, Eisenberg, drawn by the sound of the saw, has come out of his house and is hovering near his new brick barbecue pit, gauging the length of Lieberman's tree, calculating angles in his head. He looks worried.

Yesterday Segal's wife called Lieberman at home and cried about Miss Lash; later, while Sheila was watching a rerun of Outer Limits, Laura called and explained to Lieberman that it was all right for her to be seeing another man. "I don't really think I've ever been in love before," she told her father.

Lieberman makes the first cut; Eisenberg watches him. The sawdust flies; chips make a little pile on the grass. Nobody has noticed the woman who appears at the bottom of the garden, silent. She comes closer. Lieberman stands back; the wood in the notch he has made is yellow-white, looks healthy, oozes clear sap. He wonders if he's doing the right thing. He turns to go to the other side of the tree, and for the first time he sees her. "Hello," he says. He begins the back cut; he leans into the saw, watches the chain bite, the bark fly; he concentrates on his task, aware that behind him Sheila and the woman have come together and are talking easily, as if they'd known each other for years.

He told Segal's wife to be patient—it was a matter of age; Segal would come back if she gave him some room for his foolishness now. But as he talked he was remembering the glad light in his partner's eye when he looked at Miss Lash, and Lieberman felt he was telling a lie. Segal's wife doesn't have tits like oranges. The saw's motor slows and barks in a deeper tone as Lieberman cuts deeper into the trunk. Eisenberg is holding a hand over his mouth. His eyes look a little crazy.

Lieberman steps back; everything is ready to happen. He gives the tree a little push. It cracks loudly, begins to lean forward; the ropes hold, guide the slow fall. Lieberman turns to the women. "No problem," he says. "Just like in the book."

The rope on the left side breaks. The backlash catches Lieberman above the eyes like a long bullwhip; it stuns him. The tree slips to one side, away from Eisenberg and his barbecue; it catches the corner of Lieberman's house. Cedar shakes make a fountain against the blue sky, roof-timbers snap. The bathroom window falls out in one piece to lie on the grass, a long branch reaches out and topples Lieberman's chimney, another backhands the television antenna off the roof. Lieberman moans; a drop of blood falls down his nose; the forgotten chainsaw chug-chugs quietly in his left hand. Eisenberg stares. Suddenly the psychiatrist laughs, a loud quacking laugh. He looks around guiltily, clamps the hand tight over his lips and runs inside his house.

In the living-room, the woman covers the long cut on

Lieberman's forehead with surgical tape from the medicine cabinet. He sits on the couch, holding a cup of coffee, thinking *who can tell about life,* over and over, the same words singing through his head like a stuck record. *Who can tell.*

"Laura wants to come home and live for a while," Sheila says. "David's leaving her."

"Let her go and live with the other one," Lieberman says.

"She can't, Martin. He's married."

"That's just fine," Lieberman says. "That's wonderful."

The woman strokes his forehead. "Your other girl's so very different," she says. "Gets straight A's in school and you don't have to worry about her at all. That's how you were when you were her age—nobody had to worry about you."

The smell of the sawdust and sap comes through the hole in the roof. Also the sound of Eisenberg laughing again. The woman holds Lieberman's hand. "How could it be your fault? You gave her everything. You're a terrific father. Some kids just don't work out. But you did; I'm very proud of you."

I need, Lieberman thinks. *I want. I need.* What's truth compared to that?

Daddy. Lieberman practices it under his breath, no more than a thought the first time. The cut on his forehead throbs with the beat of his heart. Outside Eisenberg laughs again, an ugly duck sound. I loved that tree, Lieberman thinks. The woman touches his cheek. *Daddy,* Lieberman whispers, holding her hand tight, making up his mind.

Things I Did to Make It Possible

One. I made love to Margaret only in the missionary position. We are not baboons.

Two. I went to the ocean every chance I got. My favorite place was the Santa Monica Pier but I also went to the Malibu Pier, Topanga Beach, Zuma Beach, Newport Harbor. Sometimes I fished. Mackerel scream when they are pulled out of the water, but they probably don't feel much. Certainly they don't know what's happening to them.

Three. One of the hardest things was watching my weight. I'll never be a fat man if I can help it. Ate a lot of celery, tomatoes by the dozen, lettuce. Gobbled cucumbers just so I'd have something in my mouth.

Four. Sometimes talking to Margaret is like pissing in a violin, as my mother used to say. She listens but she doesn't believe. Still I try.

Five. I ran four miles a day around the golf course in Tarzana. Sometimes with Marty, more often alone; he's like an old man —his tits joggle sadly when he runs and he gets out of breath and asks me to stop and wait for him every few hundred yards. One leg of our course runs along the bank of the Los Angeles River, a terrible place.

Six. The tree in my back yard throws fish-shaped leaf-shadows on the patio bricks. Let a little breeze blow and clouds of shadow-fish wriggle across the bricks.

Seven. Life in a tropical paradise. Lagoon is one of the great words in the language. Listen to the sound of it. *Lagoon.* I don't know why she should be fucking Marty.

Eight. If she is. He's forty like me, and not in nearly as good a condition. What's she getting out of it? I could ask.

Nine. Another thing I did: I quit smoking.

Ten. I went to Tijuana and bought Margaret an armadillo purse with red-glass eyes. The paws curl under the hollow belly, where she can put things.

Eleven. When we were going to the university she was fucking our friend Campbell the playwright. Artsy-craftsy Campbell weighed about ninety pounds and came up to my shoulder, but he had an agile mind. And a way with women.

Twelve. I loved my wife.

Thirteen. Help me, Dr. Eisenberg. You comedian, you.

Fourteen. Margaret has to my knowledge slept with: Campbell, Marty, myself. I think she also went to bed with Norman Haas at least once. He had polio and is even smaller than Campbell. He can only move one arm, and not all of that. The woman is a saint, possibly, in her own view.

Fifteen. I also bought some armadillo boots for myself. Armadillo babies. God but that's sad. I'm wearing their mama on my feet.

Sixteen. We are nature. The smog is nature. I tried to learn to love it. I sucked it in deep when I ran, and made it a part of myself. Listened to the golf-balls whizzing in the cottonwood leaves above my head and took deep breaths. Jumped over small snakes. Told myself that by the time I was ready to die it would seem natural to me. Maybe necessary. Conceivably beautiful.

Seventeen. Here are some things I collected during this time and did not use: a French postcard of a woman with bare breasts and one eye closed to indicate sexiness; a 1941 Buick with side-mount spare wheels and burned valves; an Italian coin made out of aluminum; a black pebble from the beach, cut in half by a clear streak of quartz; a dried blowfish from the souvenir shop on Santa Monica Pier; a sterling-silver medal of Benjamin Franklin; the white skull of a small animal with long front teeth.

Eighteen. I went for long walks at night and thought about the world.

Nineteen. We are not baboons or dogs. Something else.

Twenty. Fourteen years? Almost exactly now. It seems like no time at all since we were all innocent in Tucson.

Twenty-one. I picked up a little girl hitch-hiking on the corner of Sunset and Doheny, and drove her out to Zuma Beach.

Twenty-two. What's this life all about anyway?

Twenty-three. In general I tried. I think I can say that much. I loved the smog; I loved the yellow grass that looks dead on the hillsides from the middle of May onward; I loved the long loose whips of the freeways that connect this town; I loved the Santa Ana wind that makes the best of us crazy; I loved the rain in winter.

Twenty-four. Try to be an angel—see where it gets you.

Twenty-five. Sweet little girl from somewhere back East. She blew me under one of the lifeguard towers in the middle of the night and we talked until the sun came up while I snoked her cigarettes and listened to the surf. Boom-boom-boom. Saddest goddamn sound on earth.

Twenty-six. I had trouble with the video portion of my life. I kept fading in and out.

Twenty-seven. I gave money to: the City of Hope; Muscular Dystrophy; United Good Neighbors; the Heart Fund; the Cancer Society; the Boy Scouts of America; two little Mexican girls who came to the front door selling scented candles; my hitch-hiker.

Twenty-eight. A dream where my father was a small blue pyramid with a single brown eye, like the picture on the dollar-bill. In my sleep he seemed perfectly natural in that form. We carried on a long conversation about life. I'm not a big-time dreamer; not many of the dreams that I can remember are as strange as that, or as interesting. Usually it's the old naked-in-a-crowd-of-strangers, or flying-over-the-hills sequence. Now and then I dream of a golden girl and love so tender I wake up with tears on my face.

Twenty-nine. Eisenberg said I should expect to feel like this. Then he laughed like a duck.

Thirty. I'm not a bigtime *anything*. Not strictly true. I want. I'm a bigtime wanter, maybe.

Thirty-one. I told the girl what I had to have if I was to keep going. Love, warmth, not to be alone. She touched me. No, not that, I said. You don't understand. Yes I do, she said. Lie back and listen to the water.

Thirty-two. I drove her all the way to Santa Barbara and left her by the side of the highway, under the big fig tree on Anacapa Street. Where was she going from there? I don't think she knew for sure. Should I have made myself responsible for her? Not left her to work her way up the coast? Not picked her up in the first place, when I knew what was going to happen because I wanted it, because she wanted it? I don't suppose I'll ever know.

Thirty-three. I took Margaret and Marty to dinner at the Yellowfingers on Ventura Boulevard. I got them both drunk, and then I picked a fight with the waitress for no earthly reason at all, and then I got up and went home and left Marty and Margaret to straighten it all out. I don't think either one of them could walk or say a straight sentence after all the Manhattans I made them drink.

Thirty-four. I sat under my tree and watched the fish-shaped leaf-shadows drift across the bricks. I've had no luck in my life.

Teller, the Bear and
The Yellow Thunderbird

Teller and God lived together in the house Teller's TV series had built, high on a ridge at the east end of Beverly Hills. Teller had found God scratching at the front door one morning and had taken him in because he didn't like cats. Teller had a theory that living with somebody or something you disliked was good for the constitution; it kept you toned up, gave you a keen spiritual edge, made you humble. After a while he got to like God and changed his mind about cats, but he kept him anyway, for company.

Teller's mother lived by herself in a condominium ten miles south of Laguna Beach. Her living room was long and narrow, and the small end was closed by a glass wall. Sitting in it was like sitting in the bottom of a gun barrel pointed square at the Pacific. Teller hadn't gained a pound since his television days, but he was a big man, and when he came to visit his mother always made him sit in the one chair; she had bought it especially to hold his two hundred and forty pounds. After two or three drinks he sometimes caught himself clutching the steel arms so he wouldn't roll down the length of the room and tumble into the dark-blue sea.

"Love," his mother said. "It's the most important goddamned thing in the world. It's a tragedy you don't know that."

"But I do know it," Teller said.

"Never mind," his mother said. "It'll come to you in time then you'll see. What you ought to worry about now is your house. If you don't stir yourself and pay the taxes they'll take it away from you and give it to some Arab."

"Not for a while," Teller said.

He reaffirmed his grip on the chair and stared out to sea. A crossing wind was complicating the waves and the sun flashed off the crests with painful, unpredictable brightness. Teller's eyes stung, but he disciplined himself and kept staring until the tears came. "They can't sell me out for five years after I stop paying taxes; it's only been three."

His mother was a small woman with a terrible will. Teller's father had had to leave home a long time ago. She stood ramrod straight, six inches in front of the wall, looking down at her son. She was no sloucher; Teller had never seen her lean on anything. Above her head an iron rack held her three favorite guns: an over and under shotgun with twin triggers, a more manageable side-by-side she used for skeet competition, and the M-1 Garand that Teller's father had brought back from the War, which she had learned to shoulder and shoot like an expert. She belonged to the Laguna Beach Police Ladies' Auxiliary and fired on their range the second Tuesday of every month.

"And why don't you get rid of those damned animals?" she said.

Deer came out of the Santa Monica Mountains to feed on Teller's bushes in the dry season, rattlesnakes lived under his rocks near the edges of the property, and sometimes a coyote came down to see what he could see. But his mother didn't mean any of those; she was talking about Bear, who lived out back of the house in a big round steel cage most of the time, and whom she pluralized for the sake of argument. Or maybe she meant he had to get rid of God too, Teller thought.

Bear and Teller liked to wrestle on the lawn in the morning, while God sat in his tree, remote from the commotion below. Bear wasn't big, as bears go, but she outweighed Teller by more than two hundred pounds and she always won, though Teller was in good shape, as solid as when he'd been on the series. After the game, if it was a hot day, Teller turned on the sprinklers and Bear lay paws in the air on her back under the arcs of falling water, looking happy as hell.

"You threw away your career," Teller's mother said. "And now you live in a damn zoo. You could have been as big as anybody and you threw it out the window. Would you at least tell me why?"

He was on his fourth Jim Beam and water, and his mother's living room looked more like a cannon to him than ever; any second now this big gun might go off and shoot him in a smoky parabola out over the water. He closed his eyes.

"Marge," he said. "Stop. You don't have any idea what you're talking about."

"The other day in the recreation room I met four different people who remember you from the series. One lady said you had more sex appeal than John Wayne."

"John Wayne?"

"All right, she said Tab Hunter. But it's the same thing."

"Practically," Teller said.

"What about the car, if you won't go back to work?" his mother said. "It's a part of television history, and some people would give a lot of money to have it. At least enough for you to pay your back taxes on the house." She frowned at Teller. "Arabs," she said. "I don't know why they let them come here anyhow. They're ruining the country."

"Let the car sit," Teller said. "It's fine where it is."

"It's not as if you ever took it out of the garage. Tell me when was the last time you drove it? It's up on blocks and the wheels are off it. I looked in the window."

"Do you know anything about cars?" Teller said.

"I never cared for them at all, you know that. They were your father's hobby, not mine."

"This one's ruined from sitting there so long already," Teller said. "I couldn't drive it if I wanted to." He got up, careful to keep his eyes turned away from the ocean, and poured himself another drink. His head felt unnaturally clear.

"I loved the stories," his mother said. "Every week you saved somebody. Like Maverick. They had writers in the industry in those days."

"*Maverick* was a comedy," Teller said.

"You looked so goddamned handsome in those opening shots, rolling down the road with the convertible top folded down. I was proud enough of you to bust. How old were you then?"

"Twenty-eight."

"Every woman I know was in love with you."

"I wish you'd stop talking about it. It's embarrassing. That's all over, Marge."

"How old are you now?" his mother said. "Forty? If I was

forty I'd show the world a thing or two."

"You're not old," Teller said. He laid a hand on her arm and took it away again.

"So what are your plans? How are you going to get yourself out of this hole?"

"I don't need any plans," Teller said. "And I'm not in any hole. I'm happy the way I am."

"It's that damn bear," his mother said.

"What's Bear got to do with it?"

"You think it loves you but all it cares about is the meat you feed it every day." She took his arm. "It sleeps with you in your bed sometimes—I've seen hairs. Are you going to deny that?"

"We're friends," Teller said.

"An animal," his mother said. "It stinks. Everything around your house stinks from bear. I'm surprised the neighbors haven't complained; they're probably waiting for you to come to your senses. It's got to stop, can't you see that?"

"I know," Teller said. "I ought to get married, right?"

"Your father was a son of a bitch. I wouldn't wish a marriage like mine on anybody." She looked down at Teller tenderly. "But you're not like Walter," she said. "Thank God you're not a damn bit like your father. The only thing he loved was his damn cars. You can love—you have love in you."

Three days after that she broke into his garage, took a jack out of the trunk and started to put the wheels back on the yellow Thunderbird. Teller didn't know anything was wrong until he went down the path to pick up his mail and saw the garage doors hanging open. He stuck his head inside; she had already bolted the back wheels on. The jack was under the front bumper, slowly lifting the corner of the car off the cinder-blocks. His mother was putting all her ninety-five pounds on the jack handle and she didn't know Teller was standing behind her until he opened his mouth.

"What are you doing?"

She didn't even turn her head. "Should have done it a long time ago." She pumped the handle steadily. The car rose in little jerks.

"Stop," Teller said.

"I'm going to put this automobile on the road. I don't care if you drive it or sell it, but I can't stand the idea of something like this sitting in your garage being no use to anybody."

"The battery's been dead for years. It's got no brakes. It's been sitting so long all the little rubber seals have rotted out. It isn't safe even if you could get it started."

"If you won't help me, don't get in my way," she said.

"Marge."

"I *will* do it," she said. "Your life isn't over; I'm not going to let you bury yourself. I'll do what has to be done."

He had to pick her up and carry her up the brick path to the patio. He set her down in a lounge chair; she let herself be handled without complaining, but he could tell from the way she breathed that she was furious. He went inside to fetch her a drink; when he came out she had gotten up out of the chair and was prowling the edges of the patio, peering between the trees, lifting her nose to smell the air.

"Where is it?" she said.

"Where is what?"

"You know damn well."

"She's in her cage out back."

His mother sat down. "You think I'm crazy don't you?" she said. "You're the one who's crazy. I could have you certified, you know that? I could call Eisenberg tomorrow and they'd come and take you away." She looked at the drink in her hand and set it back on the table. "I just might do it," she said. "I'd be doing you a favor."

She called him twice from Laguna Beach and didn't mention the bear or the yellow Thunderbird. The third time she called she invited him to dinner and told him to dress decently, so that he knew she had invited a girl for him. "Coat and tie?" he said.

"At least some clean Levis. God knows I don't expect a hell of a lot from you. Just don't show up drunk."

The girl's name was J. J. Turner and she didn't ask Teller any embarrassing questions about his days on the series, or why he didn't act any more. When dinner was over he dragged his chair the length of the living room and sat against the glass wall with his back turned to the sea. J. J. sat on the carpet and leaned against his knees; she had long blonde hair combed straight and severe, a round pretty face and green eyes. Teller knew he ought to be feeling at least a casual kind of lust, but J. J. looked too small to him to sustain such feelings.

"She's in the industry," Teller's mother said. Teller leaned forward in his chair and stared down at the blonde hair, waiting for the rest.

"She writes for television; I bet you've seen some of her shows."

Teller stood up. J. J. looked at him and smiled down at her reassuringly. "She's done scripts for all the big ones," his mother said. *"Rockford Files, Police Story, Baretta."*

"I have to go home now," Teller said. He moved toward the door. His mother blocked him.

"They're always looking for good actors," she said.

Teller sidestepped past her. On the front steps he turned back and shook hands with J. J. "I'm sorry about Marge," he said. "I don't think she can help it."

The next morning, through a blanket of sleep, he heard heavy intent hammering. He ignored it; it persisted, became louder, stopped. He sat up and looked out the window. The garage faced away from him but he caught a glimpse of something big and yellow moving silently down the slope of the driveway toward the street.

By the time he reached his gate, still trying to zip up his pants on the run, the Thunderbird had rolled out of sight. This time his mother had used a crowbar and a sledgehammer; the new bigger lock Teller had put in was lying on the sidewalk next to the mailbox along with her tools.

"Marge!" He made a megaphone out of his hands and called again. "Marge! Stop!" He thought she probably couldn't by now. The road fell sharply to Beverly Glen in a series of hairpins and S-curves; the sidewalks were narrow, and eucalyptus trees grew out of them every few yards. Teller started running. She must have figured she could start the engine if she got the car going fast enough. He thought he heard a squeal of tires ahead of him;

though she didn't like cars, she was a good driver—maybe she'd make it all the way to the bottom of the hill, through the curves and past the trees poised on the edge of the road like clubs. Then she would have to have the good sense to point the car uphill toward the mountains and let it roll to a stop; he knew there were no brakes at all. He heard another squeal, louder and deeper-pitched. He ran faster. When he heard the crash he pulled up, then he started down the hill again, walking slowly.

The Thunderbird had poked its nose through a cedar fence; a wrought-iron lamp-post lay across the hood. Teller's mother was behind the wheel; she looked unhurt except for a bloody nose. She dabbed at it with a tissue, leaning over so she wouldn't get blood on her dress.

"Somebody had to do it," was the first thing she said to him. "You would have let it sit in the garage another ten years until it was nothing but rust—you can't tell me different."

The impact had jammed the driver's door shut and he had to brace his foot against the side of the car and yank on the handle to let her out. His tennis shoe left a muddy print on the yellow paint. His mother walked with him slowly around the car; one front wheel was cockeyed, the windshield was cracked, the radiator dribbled water. "Look at this goddamned car now," she said.

"I suppose you'll try to tell me it's my fault," she said when they had walked back to Teller's patio; they drank coffee and waited for the wrecker to come pick up the Thunderbird. "What is it with you?" she said. "Your father was a cold fish, but you're not. I can see you love these damned animals. Why can't you love something human? What was wrong with J. J.?"

*   *   *   *

Teller's mother crouches in the bushes above his house, nearly at the top of the ridge, hidden from below by dusty leaves. She stares at her son through a pair of binoculars. At her feet lies the heavy M-1 rifle with a clip already loaded; the bolt is closed, a round in the chamber.

Down on the lawn Teller is playing with Bear; God sits in the tree licking his face. Teller's mother picks up the rifle and draws a bead on the bear, then she puts it down and tests the wind by dropping a pinch of dry grass and watching which way it falls, how far it travels. She adjusts her rear sight two clicks to the left and aims again. The front sight wanders left, edges back and settles on Bear's chest.

But the picture won't hold. Bear disappears from the sights and is replaced by Teller—first his arm, then the shoulder, finally his face. Then it's Bear's turn, but the animal slips away and Teller's mother finds herself staring down the barrel of the M-1 at her son again.

"Shit," she says. She puts down the heavy gun and wipes her forehead with a hankie that smells of lavender.

Teller is pinned down by Bear; he throws himself from side to side to break her hold, but her weight presses him deeper and deeper into the soft grass. The raunchy wild-animal smell of her makes him dizzy; it seems to Teller that the sun is swinging in great loops and Einsteinian figure-eights in the sky; in spite of the four hundred and fifty pounds of brute on top of him he suddenly feels light as an angel.

"Uncle!" he cries. Immediately Bear rolls off and sits up, grinning at him. "One of these days I'm going to get tough with you," Teller tells her lovingly. "And we'll see who does the grinning then."

The first shot sounds to Teller like the time when he was four years old and his mother suddenly slapped him on the ear; it comes to him as pain. He looks around and sees the muzzle flash as his mother fires the second time. He thinks he might be hit, and feels himself all over with questioning hands, but doesn't find a wound. He doesn't think to lie down and make himself less a target, but goes on sitting, stupidly exposed. He hears another shot, or rather he hears the meat-cleaver sound of the bullet hitting flesh. Blood slowly runs down Bear's chest; it loses itself quickly in the rough brown hair. Bear looks puzzled; she claws away the pain, grins at Teller. She slowly lies down on her side; another shot drills the space where she just was and makes the bark fly on a eucalyptus behind her. Another, better aimed, carves a long furrow in Bear's hide. The hair and skin, as if surprised, peel back slowly, after the echoes of the shot have died away. Blood swells out of the cut, dark and certain. The wound is as straight and regular as if someone in a bear suit had pulled a zipper to let himself out.

God jumps down from his branch and walks stiffly up to where the man still sits. Teller reaches out to touch the cat. "It's all right," he says mechanically. The next shot snatches God from under his hand, breaks the animal in midair and tosses him away into the oleanders.

From up on the ridge there comes the long-drawn out twang of the empty clip ejecting automatically from the rifle; it seems to Teller that the sound is lasting forever, dying and swelling like the whine of a tuning-fork held too close to the ear.

A bitter cry follows, full of triumph and sorrow.

"Now you'll have to love something human, Teller. Love something human, why can't you?"

Drowning in California

Out here everything is possible. Last year I was Tony Bill's secretary, the year before that I lived with my mother in Manhattan, this year I'm writing a screenplay about Howard Hughes that's going to sell for two hundred thousand dollars.

My agent says it's a cinch, a sure-fire sale as soon as I get it done. He has a house on the beach near where Topanga Creek comes out of the canyon and spills itself in the ocean. He believes in the power of the pyramids; he has one made out of redwood two-by-fours over his bed, the point right up against the ceiling. He calls me sweet Georgia and wants to take me to bed underneath his pyramid to demonstrate the power; I haven't let him yet.

People swim in the nude fifty feet from Peter's back porch: healthy Californians with perfect bodies. They come nearer once the sun goes down and defecate in his vegetable garden; he has to go out there and clean up with a little scoop-shovel every morning. Peter has a perfect body and a wrinkled face which has no character at all. He runs five miles on the beach every day barefoot; sometimes he gets ecstatic and forgets to watch out for the little piles of shit.

2

Wednesday nights my best friend Alice and I go to our therapy group in the basement of Richard's house on Hollywood Boulevard. He shares the house with his father Maxwell Birnbaum, the paperback psychologist. Max's books sell by the million; he's been on the *Tonight Show* and Johnny Carson called him a genius and let him kiss Dolly Parton. Max is about five feet tall; his head looked like a coconut wedged between two cantaloupes. I've noticed that Richard's voice gets a little tense when he talks about his father, and he looks up at the ceiling. The old man pads around up there during our sessions, working on his next book. Richard says it's going to be called PASSIVE AGGRESSION AND THE LOVE-GAME. I had to go up and use the bathroom once because the downstairs toilet was stopped up; when I came out I caught a glimpse of Max through the open door. He was sitting naked as a monkey in front of his IBM, scratching himself. The only thing he wore was a pair of chrome-rimmed glasses. He started to turn his head and I ducked back down the stairs.

Richard says there is no such thing as morality or immorality, only certain behaviors we might want to change because we weren't comfortable with them.

"What if I was comfortable about killing somebody?" I said.

"That would be your own trip," Richard said. "Remember what Camus and Ken Kesey said—'If you feel like kicking ass, kick ass.' "

"Camus said that?"

"That's what he meant," Richard said.

When we went outside for a break I elbowed Alice. "He's dumb," I said. "But Jesus isn't he gorgeous."

"Everybody falls in love with their therapist," she said.

"Don't act superior. If you'd sat any closer to him you would have been in his lap. And the way you stared at his chest was embarrassing."

She took one of my cigarettes and waited for me to light it; she's an old-fashioned girl and expects people to do things for her. "Embarrassing to who?" she said.

"Come on, Alice," I said.

"Come on, Georgia." She said it in her sweetest honeysuckle-flower-of-the-South voice. She flipped the cigarette away into somebody's bushes.

"Aren't you afraid you'll start a fire?" I said.

"Sprinklers," she said. "Everybody has sprinklers."

3

Alice and I discuss everything but I don't always tell her the absolute truth. Stanley calls me nearly every night and I talk to him for a while before I hang up. Why shouldn't I? It's a human voice. He doesn't say much when we're together but on the phone he sounds like a regular person. But if I told Alice I talked to Stanley she'd laugh. She has a mean laugh. Another thing I don't know if I like about her is her Southern accent; when she came out here she was still a kid but she drove out from Tennessee with her whole family: uncles and cousins and aunts. She never did lose that twangy way of talking. She lets every word trail out of her mouth until it dies a natural death. Sometimes I almost think I'm going to go crazy waiting for her to finish a sentence.

"I don't even like Stanley," I told her. "I wish you'd quit bringing him up. I don't know why I let him make love to me."

If you can call it that; he twittered inside me for about five seconds and then drove me home as fast as he could.

"He's so *ugly*," she said. "He doesn't even have a body. Did you ever look at his arms? They're nothing but little skinny white sticks."

It was your standard Valley winter morning, with clouds thin as gauze streaming across from West to East, from Malibu where the beautiful people live. A little round sun about as big as a grapefruit showed through now and then. Malibu is where I'm going to live as soon as Peter sells the screenplay. I'll run on the beach every morning with a big dog, and make *my* body beautiful.

In the early morning when the writing isn't going very well because my characters insist on saying stupid things, I turn on *Sesame Street* and look past the TV at the clouds. It's either *Sesame Street* or the morning news and at eight o'clock I'm not ready for Jerry Brown and Jane Fonda and the Hillside Strangler. So I watch the little kids dance around and learn their numbers. I like Big Bird. I like Oscar. I can't stand Ernie because of his awful laugh. He reminds me of Stanley; it's the laugh and the funny clump of hair standing out on top of his head.

"He drives a Mercedes," I told Alice.

She looked at me. "Is that where you made it with him?"

I blushed. "Yeah."

"Oh God," she said. "That's so tacky."

"We were parked on Mulholland Drive," I said. "Did you ever see the view of the Valley from up there? I don't think I was paying attention; anyway I was stoned."

"How old are you?"

"Twenty-seven."

"I haven't done that since I was fourteen," she said.

"You know us New Yorkers," I said. "And it isn't Stanley's fault he doesn't have a place of his own. He has to take care of his mother because she's sick."

"Tacky," Alice said. "Very tacky."

"Let's change the subject," I said.

"I bet now he calls you up all the time and moons at you over the phone."

"He called once and I told him to quit bothering me. Who needs somebody like Stanley?"

"Nobody's done it in the back seat of a car since beach-blanket movies," Alice said. "Haven't you got any pride?"

"Front seat," I said. "We did it in the front seat. Not that it makes any difference."

"I bet he's younger than you are too," Alice said.

"Let's drop it," I said. "I think I'll go for a swim."

"You're crazy. The pool isn't even heated."

"So I'll catch pneumonia."

"You'll get cramps and drown."

"Stick around and rescue me," I said. "You'll get on the news."

"Forget it," Alice said. "I don't want to watch anybody die. Anyhow I've got an audition this afternoon. I think I'll go curl my hair."

Her voice reminded me of fat bumblebees droning in phony eternal sunlight. When I was a kid I spent my summers with an old aunt in Bethany Beach, Delaware. The boys used to tease me about my New York way of talking fast and I tried to learn to drag out my words the way they did, but I never quite got the hang of it. I didn't date and I did crazy things without knowing why. One time I remember I floated out from the beach on an innertube and fell asleep and damn near drowned. When I woke up the beach was so far away it wasn't much more than a line on the horizon. I looked at it for a long time before I decided it was worth it to try and paddle back.

4

Peter took me to a screening at Paramount. In the picture bugs came out of a crack in the ground after an earthquake. They looked like ordinary big black beetles, a little larger than life, until they got upset, then they glowed red-hot and set fire to what they were standing on. The main character had one crawl in his ear while he was asleep; when it started to glow he jumped up and bounced off the bedroom walls, waving his arms while the beetle quietly burned a hole into his head.

"This is the worst film I ever saw," I said.

"See that man two rows ahead of us?" Peter whispered. "That's Lynn Swann, the wide receiver for the Pittsburgh Steelers."

"I bet he's not having much fun either," I said.

It was still light when we got out, one of those California evenings that seem to hang on and on forever, and we went back to his house. We sat on the back porch and drank unfiltered apple juice that looked like pond water. A man on the beach was running around wearing nothing but a Superman cape. He had a tiny erection and displayed it to everybody, but I couldn't see anyone who cared.

"Frigadoon!" I said.

"What?"

"There's an old guy in our therapy group who says that all the time," I explained. "It's his favorite word."

"What does it mean?"

"I don't know; he just says it. I like the way it sounds."

I went inside for more apple juice and when I came out the sun was going down, the nude people were putting their clothes on, Superman was walking away up the beach toward Malibu. I felt so goddamned sad I wanted to cry. I tapped Peter's glass with mine. "Here's to Howard Hughes," I said. The stuff still looked like muddy water, but it tasted like fresh apples. More sadness.

"Why do people shit in your garden?" I said.

"I don't know," he said.

We sat there like that waiting for the sun to finish drowning itself in the flat sea. Peter put his hand on my leg and gave me his best sincere look.

"Want to go in the bedroom?" he said. "It'll cheer you up."

"No," I said. "You're an asshole, you know that?"

5

Stanley took me to meet his mother. We didn't talk at all on the freeway; he whistled between his teeth.

His mother was lying in bed wearing a satin dress and a hat about three feet across, with red silk roses pinned on it. Stanley is so damned ugly I can hardly believe I go places with him. Stanley the toad, Alice and I call him. His mother's maid served tea and cookies and we made conversation, or Stanley the toad made conversation with his mother and I ate cookies until I couldn't hold any more. When I can't smoke, I eat. The mother had skin as white as typing paper, and a big circle of rouge on each cheek like a clown. I liked her right away.

"Are you doing well at your job?" she asked Stanley.

"Yes, mama," he said. "Hee, hee, hee." He laughed exactly like Ernie. I wanted to reach over and slap his hair flat down on his head.

"I won't be around much longer and then you can have this big-old place all to yourself," mama said.

"The cookies are delicious," I said.

"They come from Famous Amos," she said.

"Well they're delicious," I said.

"I haven't felt well since your father died," she said to Stanley. He sighed, started to whistle between his teeth, caught her eye and stopped.

"Andrew could have been a great man in the industry if he'd had the right wife," she said. "I know I failed him."

"Hee," Stanley said. He covered his mouth with his hand.

"He once worked with Stanley Kubrick," she said. "But he took up with floozies and it killed him. I live in fear that you'll do that too."

"Let's hope not," I said.

"It was my fault," his mother said. "If I'd been more attentive to his needs—but I'm not a warm woman. I was never brought up to be."

"Do we have to talk about this, mother?" Stanley said.

"This is really woman's talk, dear. Why don't you go and walk in the garden for a while? The roses are lovely this week."

"No, listen," I said. "I'd love to stay longer, but I have to go home. I'm expecting an important call from my agent. Thank you very much for the cookies."

I made Stanley drop me off around the corner from the apartments so Alice wouldn't see the Mercedes; she's my best California friend but she doesn't have to know everything I do.

When I walked in my phone was ringing. "Where were you?" Alice said.

"I went down to the K-Mart."

"Your car wasn't gone."

"I took a bus."

"Nobody takes a bus. You were out with Stanley, weren't you?"

"Yes," I said.

"You're crazy. I could introduce you to a dozen men."

"You already have," I said. "They were all married."

"Honey they're the best kind. They don't make trouble."

"No thanks," I said. "I have to hang up now—I'm going to take a bath and do some writing."

"You and John Milton," she said. I had told her how Milton used to take a cold bath before writing a sonnet, so as to be pure in spirit.

"So what are you doing to make yourself famous?" I said. "Trying to break into TV commercials?" I stared out the window at the clouds; they were low and moved fast and I felt as if my building had broken loose from the foundations and was shooting through the sky like a balloon. Pretty soon I would be out over the desert and Los Angeles would be nothing but a line on the horizon; I would have a hell of a time getting back before I drowned.

"I'm sorry, Alice," I said.

"I shouldn't have been so pushy about Stanley the toad," she said. "Only he's such a little creep. I hate to see you wasting yourself."

"You've never seen him except for that one time when I brought him down by the pool to watch me swim. Everything you know about him is just what I told you. Maybe I lied."

"Actually that's not strictly the facts," she said. "I went out with him once, to find out what you saw in him."

"Did you go to bed together?" I said.

"Us Southern girls never kiss and tell."

"Kiss?" I said.

"Well whatever."

"I don't believe you exist," I said. "I think I made you up in my head."

"Don't get huffy," she said. "Anyhow I made him take me to the Holiday Inn on Ventura Boulevard. We had a great room; the sheets matched the wallpaper and there's a faucet in the bathroom just for icewater."

"Real class," I said. "How was it? Did he talk to you?"

"Only about his mother," Alice said.

6

I gave Peter the screenplay and went out on his back porch to give him a chance to read it without me looking over his shoulder. It's about Hughes, of course, but it's also about how wonderful everything is here, how impossible. I worked Alice into it, and Richard and Max. And Stanley.

It was a cold foggy day and no nudies were out. I looked for Superman but all I saw was a fat woman in a warmup suit jogging along the beach with her dog, and way out in the water a couple of surfers. Maybe they weren't surfers but bits of driftwood. Little dark dots rising and falling on the slow oily waves. This is a dead coast, that's one thing the matter with it. Not like Bethany Beach, where after a storm I could walk along the sand and find shark babies, crabs, amazing shells, sand dollars. All that washes up on Peter's beach is condoms and long whips of kelp with unnatural-looking knobby ends. I looked back at him through his picture-window; he had HOWARD HUGHES spread out on his red-wood-stump coffee table, holding down the pages with a chrome pyramid. I didn't like the way he was reading; he was going too fast. My script isn't *The Golden Bowl* or anything, but it deserved better than this forty-year-old freaky-minded agent who believed in the Rosicrucians and the Libertarian Party. He has blond hair down to his shoulders and a face full of soft lines. I can't figure out how it's possible for a man's face to have so many grooves and dents and no character at all. California, I guess. I tried to work him into the story, but everything he said came out dumb. Howard Hughes wouldn't have tolerated Peter around him for ten minutes. I had to pull him like a bad tooth and fill in the gaps with an old boyfriend named Tom, who seduced me while I was Tony Bill's secretary. I found out later he slept with me so I could tell him what was happening to the scripts he turned in to Tony. That's the sort of enterprise Hughes would have loved. Tom fit right into the story.

I went into Peter's bedroom, took off my clothes and lay down in his bed, under the pyramid; if there was any occult power coming down from the two-by-fours I didn't feel it. I pulled the covers over myself and thought about gorgeous Richard and his naked father pad-padding softly upstairs during our sessions. Those chrome spectacles made him look like a '57 Oldsmobile. I thought about the terrible things I had said to Alice the last time I saw her.

Peter woke me up touching my shoulder. "Want to make out?" he said.

"Make out?" I was still half-asleep; I had dreamed about the red-hot beetles coming out of the ground. Somehow Lynn Swann had got in the dream, too. My ear hurt—I stuck my finger in it, half-afraid I'd feel little mandibles. There wasn't anything there except the hole of my ear. I started laughing.

"What's funny?" Peter drew back his hand; he was afraid of me. *"Make out,"* I said.

"Why not?" he said. "We're friends."

"You know who I'd like to make out with?" I said. "Kermit."

"Kermit?" Peter was lost.

"In my big brass bed," I said. "He's witty. He's a charmer. He'd make it playful."

"Are you feeling all right?" Peter said. "I liked the screenplay."

"Don't pout," I said. "He's a great frog. You have no call to be jealous. Would you like to hear a funny story?"

"Sure." He sat down across the room from me.

"It's hot in here," I said. I threw back the covers. He leaned forward in his chair.

"Wow," he said. "You have a terrific body."

"Shut up," I said. "Let me tell you the story. I have this girl-friend named Alice." I told him about Alice and Stanley, and the Holiday Inn, and Stanley's mother. "I made love to him once in the front seat of his Mercedes, and another time in his room, but we had to be careful not to make noise because his mother doesn't sleep."

"Never?" Peter said.

"How the hell would I know?" I leaned back on his pillow and put my hands behind my head. "Sit back and relax," I said. "We'll make out later. If I feel like it."

"How can you be so cold?" Peter said.

"Pyramid power," I told him. "I'm in the magic spot; the rays focus right here. I have the strength of ten. Now be quiet."

"I want to make it with you," Peter said.

"Later," I said. "Or maybe never. I'd have to be in the mood."

"Please," he said.

"No."

"You know what they call women like you?"

"Yes," I said. "Listen to me now. Last Sunday Alice took Stanley to Las Vegas and married him. They came to my apartment at three in the morning so I could congratulate them."

"I don't understand," Peter said. "Did you have a thing for Stanley?"

"God but you're dumb," I said. "If I was in love with Stanley it wouldn't be a funny story."

7

"Listen," I said to Richard Wednesday night, "what is it with this California? Is everybody here crazy or what?" Richard's basement is full of butterfly chairs that fold you back and relax you whether you want it or not. Passive-aggressive furniture. I tried to sit up, but it was too much of an effort.

"Don't you like it here?" Ed's wife said.

"I love it," I said.

"Frigadoon!" Ed said.

"Why don't we explore that for a minute?" Richard said.

"Explore what? Frigadoon?"

Richard raised the back of his head from *his* butterfly chair and looked at me patiently. I wanted to kiss him and hold his head on my lap. I wanted to tell him not to worry about his father. Max could kiss Dolly Parton a thousand times and still be a schmuck.

"Sorry," I said.

"When you say *crazy,* what do you feel?" he said. "Are you talking about sex?"

"Why should I be talking about sex?"

"Because sex is important," he said.

"I'll drink to that," Ed's wife said.

"So why don't we do it once in a while?" Ed said.

"One person at a time," Richard said. "We're dealing with Georgia's problem now."

" 'Sweet Georgia Brown,' " I said. That was the tune Stanley whistled all the way to his mother's house in the Mercedes.

"I want to say something," Alice said. "I think Georgia's trying to avoid her feelings by being sarcastic."

"How do you feel about that?" Richard said.

"Thank you Alice," I said.

"I think we should have a minute of silence now," Richard said.

We all sat back like obedient kids and stared at the ceiling. Max was padding around up there between stretches at the typewriter. There was a thump, as if he'd tripped over something, and Richard blinked.

"For God's sake," I said. "He's only your father."

They ignored me. The other couple in our group held hands and looked deep into each other's eyes. On weekends they go to Sandstone and make love in a big room full of mattresses with several dozen people watching. I'm twenty-seven years old and Peter says I'm a total innocent. He says that's what he loves about me and what makes my writing good. The minute began to feel like it was going to stretch forever.

"Thirty seconds more," Richard said. He must have seen my lips move.

"What if I have to say something right now?" I asked the group.

"Sshh," Richard said.

I stood up out of my chair too fast and all the blood went shooting down to my feet. I had to grab a post and hang on until my eyes cleared. Everybody looked at me.

"I don't think I can take it any more," I said. "I mean, what are we doing here?"

"Therapy," Richard said.

"I don't mean here," I said. "I mean *here*."

8

So I did a final draft of the screenplay and Peter sold it to Twentieth-Century for two hundred thousand dollars. Everything is possible. They want Tony Bill to play the part of young Howard Hughes. I bought a house on the beach, with a big glassed-in veranda that faces the ocean. I went to the SPCA and found a Great Dane named Orphan. I went to Bullock's of Wilshire and bought a dozen jogging suits. Peter asked me to marry him and I had to drink three glasses of water before I could stop laughing. It hurt his feelings and he locked himself in the bathroom with his wall-posters of Mae West until I went home. I owe money on the house but I have a contract and an advance on my next script, which I am going to call THE END OF THE WORLD IS LOS ANGELES. Yesterday I turned on the "Tonight Show" and saw Max and Richard kissing each other; Ed McMahon wiped away a tear.

Stanley's mother died. Superman lives next door; I sit in my glassed-in veranda and watch him dance on the beach in his little cape. He's asked me over to dinner Monday night.

Superman (Georgia's Dream)

The Man of Steel is tired. It's been a long time since he was that kid growing up on a Kansas wheat farm. Too many bank-robberies foiled by his super-speed, old ladies plucked from in front of speeding taxis, villains yanked out of the black smelly sewers of Metropolis, rogue missiles deflected at the last second from the Empire State Building or the Pentagon. Not to mention all that schlepping back and forth from the earth to the moon to save the space program, which would have taken some of the snap and sparkle out of a younger man. The blackouts from those little pieces of Kryptonite that turn up about once or twice a year were bound to start adding up after a while too. It's got to where he can't look at a phone booth any more without his back starting to hurt.

Even Lois is getting old, though she is still the most beautiful woman he's ever seen. She's turning a little gray and she's gone back to wearing a bra again after those wonderful years in the sixties when watching her jump up from her typewriter was enough to make him feel like a young horny Kansas high-school kid again. They've had their good times—not everything can be told in the comic-books—but a man wants to settle down. There comes a time when a quick interlude between hoisting the doomed bathysphere out of the Marianas Trench and lending a hand with a falling bridge isn't enough to satisfy. Even the occasional get-away-from-it-all weekend in her penthouse with breakfast in bed and Lois wandering around in the pink negligee he bought her last Christmas doesn't really do it for him any more. He wants something more durable.

"Did you know that Jimmy Olsen's going to be a grandfather?" he says.

Lois stops to look at him lying on his back in her queen-size waterbed. He's naked except for the sheet pulled up to his waist and even after all these years the sight of him makes her quiver a little.

"Yes I knew," she says. "He's been telling everybody around the office for six months. Are you trying to say something?"

"Nothing," he says. "I know we can't have children."

"We probably could. It was your idea not to try."

He sighs. "Even if they turned out ordinary kids what kind of a normal life could they have with their father being Superman?"

She sits down on the bed beside him. "And if it turned out that they had your powers . . ."

"They'd have no choice but to take up the trade," he says. "It hasn't been that bad, but I couldn't wish it on my kids."

She strokes his head. "Poor Clark." She's known about the secret identity for a long time—how could she not?

"You've done a lot of good things," she says. She leans toward him and the negligee falls open a little.

She still looks fine, he thinks. Always has. There was one time in Zanzibar, right after he'd saved an African States Ministers meeting from a Chinese assassination team, but other than that he's been faithful. He hasn't had much free time to fool around, that's true, but also he hasn't really wanted to. The time in Zanzibar was an exception such as happens to everybody. After he lifted the ministers to safety he locked up the Chinese hit-men in a bamboo cage and thought *well now what?* And the only answer he could come up with was: *more of the same.* Like one fire sale after another, shoving the merchandise at people who couldn't care less, never really getting ahead of the game, because that isn't the kind of game it is, until one day the heart goes, or a blood vessel in the head pops, or in his case until one more piece of Kryptonite held in front of his eyes folds him up like a Xmas card and air-mails him to the dead-letter office.

So for the first and only time he said to hell with it, scooped up the girl in his arms (she loved it—snuggled her head against the big red S) and carried her to a tight white beach on the west side of Madagascar. They spent three days together making awkward love in the sand and eating fish he snatched out of the sea with super-speed and cooked by tuning down his X-ray vision to microwave. The girl was maybe fifteen years old and at first he was glad to listen to her babble—it was a nice change from Lois and her efficient modern-woman talk—but she really didn't have much to say and anyhow the white beach wasn't the kind of place where he could feel comfortable for long. Men work until they drop; despite his foreign origins he is American enough to know that in his bones. Before he left he set up the girl in a dress shop in Dar-es-Salaam and bought her a little annuity payable through a Swiss bank. Then he went back to Lois and didn't tell her anything, but she was sensible enough to forgive him anyway.

"If it hadn't been for you," she tells him now, "Metropolis would have been blown up half a dozen times, the President's plane would have crashed in the Atlantic, Lex Luthor would own Pennsylvania and that mad Harvard professor would have dynamited Mount Rushmore. And that was only last year."

"There's no satisfaction in it any more," he says. "In the old days I'd save the mayor as his car plunged off the bridge and I'd feel good for a week. Now it all seems the same. I never do anything *fundamental,* you know what I'm saying? It's all *fix this, patch that,* avert a disaster—I'm like the plumber you only call when the pipes break. Sometimes I wish Krypton had never blown up at all."

"You'd never have met me," Lois says.

He pulls her down on the bed beside him. "That's true." But as they start to kiss he freezes. He raises his head and listens, looking at nothing. "It's Jimmy Olsen's supersonic signal," he says. "He's in trouble."

He leaps out of bed. In one corner of the bedroom is an old-fashioned wooden phone-booth—it's the first one he slipped into for his change of identity when he came to Metropolis; it used to stand outside the *Daily Planet* office. When the company replaced it with one of those little plastic bubbles on a post, Lois bought the old booth for him. They hang the blue tights and the red cape there when he's not wearing them.

"Don't be long," Lois says wistfully. The Man of Steel blows her a kiss and dives out the window, hands outstretched in the gesture that sometimes reminds her of prayer.

When he comes back she's asleep in the big bed with her head on her arms. He lands in the room with that hop and skip and stumble that everybody in Metropolis recognizes—he's always been a little awkward at landings, like an albatross, and maybe for the same reasons. His natural medium is the air, where he can soar and nothing touches him. Up there, even now, it's still wonderful; it's only at the end of the ride, when he has to come down and do his act, his rescue, touch the ground again, that the old back pains, the dizziness, the feeling of being half a dozen different people at once, strike him and make him trip over his own feet.

He takes off the cape and the blue tights and hangs them in the booth; he gets in bed beside Lois.

"What was it this time?" she says sleepily.

"Jimmy's grand-daughter was going to be born in a traffic-jam. I had to fly the mother out. Then while I was on the way back from the hospital some idiot with a backhoe cut through a gas main in Brooklyn. I had to do a quick splice and blow away the gas or half the neighborhood could have gone up. You'd think people would be more careful."

He notices that she's not paying attention; instead she's staring past his shoulder. Her face is tense and sad.

"I've been thinking," she says. "Maybe we shouldn't see each other for a while."

He can't pretend he hasn't been expecting it. He doesn't know much about women but she's been fidgety lately, affectionate and distant by quick turns. He knew something was going to be said sooner or later. But now it's come he doesn't know how to handle it.

"Well? Aren't you going to say anything?"

"Can you imagine Jimmy a grandfather?" he tells her. "It was a beautiful baby."

She shrugs impatiently. "Come on, Clark. I'm glad for Jimmy but this is us I'm talking about. We've had it, haven't we? Can't you feel it?"

"What would you like me to say?"

"You could try to talk me out of it."

"Would that do any good?"

"No."

"It seems like Jimmy's still a little kid—has it been that long already? How long ago did he get married?"

"Aren't you going to ask me why I don't want us to see each other any more?"

"Sure. Why?"

"I don't know," she says. "It seems as if I'm measuring my life around the times when we're together. I'm just remembering the last one, or else looking forward to the next. I don't feel like I'm living. It isn't any good any more."

"We could get married," he says.

"You could have married me twenty years ago."

"Would you have given up your job on the *Planet?*"

"No," she says. "Though I guess I wouldn't have to quit now if I married you, would I? Times have changed."

"So why don't we do it?" he says.

She shakes her head. "What would be the point?"

A few months go by and they don't see each other at all except at the *Daily Planet,* where they're Clark and Lois to each other, carefully friendly. It's awkward, but not too bad. She's Business Editor now and has her own glassed-in office with a ticker-tape machine and a computer terminal; he does a city column, half human-interest, half politics. Jimmy Olsen covers the Yankees in the summer and the football Giants in the fall; he has three photographers working for him, and smokes dollar cigars. There is a whole new crop of young men and women to take Superman's picture when he saves a building from collapsing or brings down a crippled airliner to a soft landing on his outstretched arms.

But though the pictures still sometimes make the front page, it isn't the same. The grateful passengers still hold up their babies and wave, the airport chaplain blesses the Man of Steel as he leaps up and into the sky off the concrete runway lined with ambulances, but there are rumblings of discontent in Metropolis and elsewhere. An old lady in the Bronx falls off her fire-escape and dies; a rival paper says WHERE WAS SUPERMAN? Another tabloid prints an old picture of him with Lois Lane, shot through her apartment window with a 2,000 millimeter lens. A state senator talks about appointing a blue-ribbon panel to choose the most deserving cases for Superman to help out. *Ramparts* does an in-depth article on his cooperation with the FBI in the fifties. The *National Enquirer* digs up a West Virginia girl willing to hit him with a paternity suit. Her kid is eight years old and can bend horseshoes barehanded. WHO ELSE COULD BE THE FATHER?

"If he fooled around a little less, he might have time to help a few more people," the Mayor is heard to grumble to one of his cronies at a political dinner.

Superman pulls an oil tanker off the rocks in the English Channel, welds the hole in its side with a quick squeeze of his hands and burns off the floating crude before it can foul the beaches. IS SUPERMAN WORKING FOR THE SAUDIS? asks a London newspaper.

He knows that Lois is out drinking late every night with cub reporters fresh out of Vanderbilt or Tulane. He doesn't need a 2,000 millimeter lens or even his X-ray telescopic vision to know who's sharing the waterbed now. She can't be getting much satisfaction out of it, he thinks.

He's right. They're handsome, bright kids but half the time they're thinking *here I am, making it with the Business Editor,* and the other half *here I am making it with Superman's girlfriend.* For her it's like making love with somebody who's making love with an abstraction. Sooner or later even the most sensible ones end up asking her about the telephone booth.

"Clark," she says one morning, "they're beautiful young brutes, but it's like nothing at all."

He brought his coffee into her office and they watch each other drink, and try to ignore the bustle and rush on the other side of the glass walls.

"How about you?" she says. "Are you fooling around?"

"No."

"Not since Zanzibar?"

"You knew?"

"You never could lie worth a damn."

"I went back last month to see if I could find her," he says.

"And you couldn't?"

"I didn't have any trouble at all. She owns a whole string of clothing stores. She weighs two-hundred pounds, has five gold teeth and a diamond in the side of her nose."

Lois laughs and the little wrinkles around her eyes make Superman suddenly feel incredibly tender.

"Isn't life a bitch," she says.

He takes off his big horn-rim glasses and pretends to wipe them with his handkerchief; he has the feeling that unless he can keep his hands busy for the next couple of minutes he's going to ask Lois if they can get together again, give it another try, and he's not certain it would be a good idea. What if she said yes? There they'd be—nothing solved, no further ahead than they were six months ago, still swimming in the same old murky pond. He feels as if he's going to drown right now; he wipes so fast and so hard that his handkerchief bursts into flames. Only a super-inhale saves him from discovery; he sucks smoke and fire and sooty fragments into his impervious lungs to clear the air. He blushes and fans away what's left of the haze. They stare at each other.

"I haven't had an accident like that since I was a teenager," he says.

"Nobody saw. Did you burn your suit?"

He reaches across the desk to take her hand. "To hell with the suit," he says. "Lois—"

She waits for him to go on, her heart jumping in spite of herself. "Yes," she says.

But that familiar faraway look comes into his eyes. "Subway collision," he says. He's already moving toward the door, already a blur.

"Yes," she says. "Yes."

The Vanishing

Cahn gambled a dollar at a time on the blackjack table. It was late afternoon and he was the only customer; the girl who was dealing turned her cards over as intently as if Cahn's bet had been a thousand dollars and her own money at stake. She was a strawberry blonde with a slightly crooked nose and eyes that were barely too far apart; charmed by imperfection, Cahn fell in love and would have told her so if he hadn't been distracted by the cards. It seemed to him that everything hung on the turn and soft fall of the cardboard rectangles on the green felt, and he followed each revelation as if, piece by piece, his life was being laid out before him. He watched the girl's hands deftly peel a card from the top of the deck and deal it to him. Another king. He pushed the cards and his silver dollar across the table to her and waited for more cards. He knew that what he felt for the girl wasn't real love, but he didn't know how he knew it, and he couldn't have begun to explain the difference.

Finally he got up and left; he walked at random, jostled by the people plunging in and out of the casinos. He made his way down the Strip, staring up at the enormous fragile signs, concatenations of fine glass bones wired together by madmen and visionaries who had become unstrung in this city of no circumstances. Who, like Cahn, had vanished from where they belonged to reappear here.

He wandered into the Circus-Circus and sat for a while while muscular women in spangled pants flew and tumbled over his head, mocking gravity. A three-man band played music unrelated to what was going on. The trumpet-player and the drummer were barely alive, but the organist rocked and swayed as if, Cahn thought, he was sending up a passionate prayer through his machine.

He found the men's room, pissed slowly, washed his hands, turned and stared at the wall full of mirrors. Without the suit, the beard gone, he didn't recognize himself. In front of him stood a stranger in Levis, a red shirt, a cowboy hat. He touched his chin and the man in front of him did the same. "I'll be a son of a bitch," Cahn thought, "it really is me." He winked at himself. "God loves you baby," he said.

At the pay telephones he dug into his pocket for a handful of coins and dialed his home number in Los Angeles. Shana answered immediately.

"Hello?" Cahn pressed the receiver against his ear until it hurt.

"Hello?" Shana said. "Who is this?"

He hung up. "It's me," he said to the dead telephone.

The cowboy boots hurt his feet and he stumbled to the bar and sat down. "Beer," he said. At home he drank wine; he hated the taste of beer.

"Where do you end up if you keep going East from here?" he said.

"Utah," the bartender said. "I wouldn't recommend it. The man who runs the place thinks he talks to God."

"Lots of people do that," Cahn said.

"He thinks God answers."

"Some of my people used to think the same thing."

"That was different," the bartender told him. "I mean it was a long time ago. Anyhow if you're set on going to Salt Lake all you have to do is follow the Interstate. Only you won't like it."

The short red-headed girl on the next stool turned to Cahn. "Are you a Jewish man?" she said. "My best girl-friend's sister married a Jew, but he went crazy."

"It happens," Cahn said.

"Locked himself up in his room all day and all night long and studied the what-you-call-it, the Talmud?"

"Maybe," Cahn said.

"I'm telling you," the girl said. "She had to slide his meals under the door." She looked at Cahn more closely. "You don't look like a Jewish man," she said politely.

"I sell real-estate," Cahn said.

"You want to have a good time?" the girl said. "I've got a date for tonight but I could come to your room tomorrow morning."

"I'm married," Cahn said.

"What difference does that make?" the girl said. "You got fifty dollars?"

"Not really."

"You've got plastic money," the girl said. "Everybody's got credit cards."

"I'm happily married," Cahn said.

Upstairs in his room he lay down on the big double bed and watched the maladjusted television where purple and orange faces came and went like sunsets. He fell asleep and dreamed that he and Shana and the girls were trapped in a bell jar and somebody was slowly pumping all the air out. "I love you," he said in his dream, but the air was already too thin and the words didn't make any sound.

He woke up singing under his breath, *I don't give a damn / I don't give a damn*, jiggling his feet in time to the tune. He knew the song; it was his litany in time of trouble. He sang it on the freeway going home to Sherman Oaks, when he missed a sale, when his daughters turned away from him or when they came too close.

He looked down at himself and saw he still had his boots on. The pointed toes had numbed his feet; they felt like pieces of wood and the boots looked ridiculous lying on the gold bedspread. He took them off and a minute later the pain of the returning circulation made him hop up and down on the carpet like a fool. As soon as he could make himself stop, he took off the rest of his clothes and stepped into the shower; he used four of the little bars of soap to rub and scrub all the parts of himself clean.

He shaved clumsily, not having had to shave himself in seven years. He put on fresh Levis and a white shirt with mother-of-pearl snap buttons. He stopped when he came to the boots and thought with longing of the loafers, hush-puppies or Adidas he used to wear on weekends when he was still somebody else. He lifted a corner of the curtain and saw that it was still dark out; his watch said four o'clock—the shoe stores would be closed. Cahn sighed and forced his feet back into the boots. But then the pain in his toes lifted his heart, as if by suffering he could climb into a higher state. He looked at himself in the mirror and smiled: a cowboy, a stranger.

By the time the sun came up he was fifty miles east of Las Vegas, traveling fast down the highway that cuts the desert like a clumsy axe-stroke. Wide sheets of glare flew off the hood of Cahn's new truck. Behind him was Los Angeles, his family, his old self; in front of him was the shortest way out. Air whistled through the vent-windows, underneath him the big knobby tires bit the asphalt and howled, springs squeaked, and fittings rattled. Cahn endured the morning heat, the glare, the noise, like a man in a dream. He missed his Mercedes, which would have drifted in near-silence along rougher roads than this one. Riding high in the seat, rolling fast, he realized he had cut himself off from his circumstances.

Why don't I just turn this thing around and go home? he thought suddenly. He turned up the air conditioner but the best it could do was to make him feel hot and cold at the same time, like a man in a high fever. He held the wheel tight, punched himself on the leg, tried to keep his mind on the driving. As far away as he could see the land looked flat salty and poisonous, until it boiled up into ash-heap mountains at the far edge of his vision. A man in a crazy place will have crazy ideas, he told himself.

Still, if I went back we could settle it. He shook his head, punched himself again. Settle what? He and Shana had decided when they first met that marriage could be a rational thing. In a fine frenzy of loving logic they had worked out everything in advance and life had conformed to their expectations. They never quarreled. Cahn had never said a harsh word to her without taking it back immediately or apologizing, sometimes in advance. He eased the truck into the left lane, where the paving was smoother. There wasn't another car on the road; he drew a mental picture of this place seen from a mile up—the long ludicrous slash of the Interstate and the red dot of his truck moving steadily along it in what was beginning to seem like exactly the wrong direction.

Cahn lived by words; persuasion was his racket. He stopped the truck and stepped out on the sand. The heat hit him like a fist between the eyes. He walked out into the desert, unsteady on his high-heeled boots, turning his ankles in the soft sand. Words worked with everybody but Shana; no matter what he said to her he saw the same person reflected in her eyes: Cahn the salesman,

Cahn the fool. Settle it, he told himself. Settle what? He didn't know. No matter how long they talked it was always the same. He sat down in the sand facing the highway in the distance. The mountains were black, the desert gray and white; the only spot of color was his truck like an ugly red flower by the side of the road.

The morning of his disappearance he'd been sitting stuck in a long line of traffic on Reseda Boulevard. It had seemed to him that this life which was passing so quickly had become unendurable. He had turned the rearview mirror on its stalk; through the back window he had seen the rising sun hanging over smoggy Pasadena like a bomb. In front of the ominous globe floated a familiar face, worried, anxious, a frowning bearded planet. The concentric rings he saw in the iris of his eyes were, he knew from a magazine article, a sign of great stress.

The car in front of him had moved off and Cahn put his own machine in gear and followed. He had bought the Mercedes a year before and loved it the way a man may love a beautiful object that makes no demands on him. He felt best when he was driving; cruising the freeways or running the boulevards on his way to make a sale, he could make sense of things sometimes. But sooner or later he had to go home and the fragile structures he built in his head failed. He kissed Shana as if through a pane of glass; when he picked up his daughters he knew he was going to die. The world at such times was a heaving sea of strangeness on which he rode like a cockleshell man, dizzy and sick of himself.

He had turned out of the traffic at the first car-dealer he'd found. On his left a line of fat American cars sat in the sun with yellow prices on their windshields; to his right were pickup trucks, high-wheeled, painted in primary colors. Cahn opened his door, already regretting the Mercedes and at the same time feeling a fierce joy because he was going to have one less thing to love. The radio in the dealer's glass shack was playing a Waylon Jennings song. "The devil made me do it the first time," it said. "The second time I was on my own."

     *   *   *   *

A friend of Shana's believed in astral travel. Cahn lay on his back in the hot sand and followed her instructions. He closed his eyes, folded his hands across his chest and made his mind a blank. After a while he tried to imagine himself pushing from the inside against the soles of his feet; he strained to push himself out of himself, to let a disembodied Cahn come out of a hole somewhere behind his ear. A spiritual hole. Nothing happened. Locked into the body Cahn lay for a long time. He opened his eyes once when a flight of F-15s from Nellis Air Force Base cut a long flesh-wound into the sky; then he closed them again and fell into a half-awake dream of his Catskill Mountain childhood, hunting bullfrogs in Schoharie Creek and turning over rocks to find little dark-blue snakes with a startling yellow ring around their necks. God but he'd been happy then, Cahn thought. He corrected himself: not happy exactly, but certain he was on the verge of happiness.

He woke up when a shadow fell across him. "What's happening here?" the shadow's voice said.

Cahn blinked; he saw himself strangely reflected in the state trooper's silvered glasses: twin Cahns diminished and warped by the curved lenses. "I was dreaming," he said.

"You can't dream here," the trooper said. "Go back to Vegas and get yourself a motel room, or drive on."

Cahn did neither. He turned the truck around as soon as the patrol car was out of sight, but instead of stopping at a motel he cruised downtown Las Vegas until he found a pawnshop.

He paid sixty dollars for a thirty-two caliber pistol and a box of shells. "Is it accurate?" he said.

The clerk wore a purple sweater with buttons missing and a ragged hole in one elbow. He looked at Cahn without interest. "It'll shoot where you point it. That's the idea of a gun."

Cahn made a circle with his thumbs and forefingers, smaller than a man's head. "Could I hit something this big with it? From across a room?"

"Depends," the clerk said. "I could do it maybe two times out of three, but I'm a good shot. Are you?"

"Fair," Cahn said. He'd been a company clerk in the army and had qualified on the range with a forty-five automatic, but that was years ago and he hadn't handled a gun since. Shana hated them. He didn't have much confidence, if he stopped to think about it. But words, which he could use so well, wouldn't do.

A few miles before the exit to Death Valley he stopped to practice. He rode out across the sand in four-wheel drive; he felt the sagebrush crush under his wheels and listened to the unsteady rumble of the V-8. He felt invulnerable, a tank driver. When he had pushed over the highway fence and rolled into open country he had felt a lawbreaker's thrill at doing the unthinkable.

The sun beat down on him, and the hot sand burned through the soles of his boots. "What am I?" he thought. The five beer cans he'd set up for targets threw elliptical shadows on the ground; he stared at them, wanting more than this. The sharp smell of burnt powder made him dreamy; he was unable to think ahead. Cahn presevered, sweating heavily under the terrible sky.

*   *   *   *

It was after midnight when he pulled up in front of his house in Sherman Oaks. When the porchlight came on he stepped back so that Shana could study him through the peephole.

"Is it you?"

He stood still, hands at his sides. He heard her unhooking the chain, slipping back the deadbolts. As soon as he stepped into the house the old familiar smell of the place dropped over him. He stumbled. "I don't give a damn," he said aloud.

"What?"

"Where are the girls?"

"I sent them to mother's."

"Good."

He had got her out of bed. She had on her terry-cloth robe, white red and lemon-yellow. Above the bright colors her face was serious. He felt nothing except the net of old habits, familiar circumstances closing around him.

"I thought you'd been kidnapped. Why didn't you call? Where have you been? Why are you dressed like that?"

He sat down on the arm of the couch. He wanted to help her but reason and logic had been tossed out the window and he had nothing to say.

"Why the truck?" she said. "What happened to the car? Did you have an accident?"

"No," Cahn said. He had nothing to offer.

"I've been in a panic," she said. She began to cry. "I didn't know what to do. I was going to call the police."

The words fell like stones and lay in a heap between them. Soon he wouldn't be able to see her at all.

"Was it a woman?" she said.

"No."

"I'm going to call Dr. Eisenberg," she said.

"Wait," Cahn said.

She looked at him carefully through the tears. "Well?"

He leaned back and felt the pistol in his back pocket. "You're a great wife," he said. "I couldn't ask for better."

"Did you think about that?" she said. "Did you think about the girls?"

"Wait," he said. "Driving home sometimes . . ."

She waited for him to go on. "Yes?"

"I'm afraid that I'll come around the corner and find our street full of fire engines. While I was at work something terrible happened—you, the girls, the house, everything is gone." He made a gesture with his hands, showing her an explosion, a smoking hole in the heart of the suburbs, the end of everything familiar.

"I dream that I have to begin a new life," he said.

Shana stared at him accusingly. "Is that what you wanted?"

"In a way." He felt he had to be honest. "Somehow. Yes."

"Why did you come back?"

He took the gun out of his pocket and showed it to her. "Prove you love me," he said.

She reached out and touched it with her fingertips. She drew her hand back quickly. In the brilliant light that fell from the chandelier, her face was intense and beautiful. Cahn was moved. "Is it a joke?" she said.

He shook his head. "What I want," he said. He stopped. "What I wanted was for you to stand over there in front of the fireplace and let me shoot a glass off your head." He laid the gun in his lap, pointed a finger at her, cocked his thumb. "Bang!" he said.

"You're crazy," she said.

"So call Eisenberg."

"No," she said. "I'll go get a glass. We'll do it."

"Why?" Cahn said. But she was already gone.

She stood with her feet slightly apart, her eyes closed tight. She had chosen a thick tumbler and filled it to the brim with water, as if she knew exactly what Cahn had dreamed of. Reflected light made a wavering circle above her head on the textured ceiling, which was painted white as a cloud.

"No," Cahn said.

She didn't open her eyes, or show that she had heard. Cahn saw that she was willing to wait forever now. As long as it took him to decide. The pistol dangled from his right hand. In his mind's eye he saw himself shoot, the tumbler fly apart, the splash of water, the fragments of glass, bright and jagged as diamonds, that would rain down on the dark-blue carpet and lie there flashing wickedly.

"All right, then," he said. He crouched, still unsteady on the boots; he raised the gun slowly; he clamped his right wrist in his left hand for extra security. The front sight came up slowly like an exclamation point between his wife's breasts, paused at the throat, settled on her forehead. His right thumb pulled back the hammer. A stranger's thumb, he thought, staring at it.

"Here we go," he said. He thought she smiled. As Cahn began the long slow squeeze of the trigger he felt himself falling in love again.

A Grown Man

I speak eight languages; I drive a yellow pickup with a powerful radio and knobby tires that howl on the freeway; my analyst looks exactly like Shecky Greene; my son's name was David before Emily took up Indian literature in Kansas and changed his name to Kali Das. I can drive down the freeway at seventy miles an hour in my yellow truck and play Willie Nelson songs so loud I don't give a damn.

This is a grown man talking here. I'm not making a complaint; I can say I've had it good. And I know language is a bitch; speak one, speak eight—we'll lie in all of them.

My department chairman keeps a brass hula dancer on his desk. She has a light-bulb screwed into the top of her head; when he throws the switch the light goes on and the girl swings her articulated hips in a slow sexy dance. His secretary wears Levis with flowers on the pockets, and a leather vest. She looks like Jean Harlow. When his door is locked in the later afternoons he's either writing one of his movie scripts or having her on the couch.

Tom thinks that people who come to see him will take the hula-girl as a joke on modern times. He likes to give me advice. "Eli," he says, "you've got to take hold of yourself or you'll never amount to anything." His eyes follow the movement of the brass hips. "But if you don't care, I don't care," he says. "It's all vanity."

The man I was twenty-two years ago went to Kenyon College with the man Tom was twenty-two years ago. Today it's all we can do to recognize each other. In those years Tom was an Apollo, an athlete with curly hair, flashing eyes and a self-conscious jock's way of walking. The girls still love him now, but he's beginning to look like hell.

When I go see him in his condominium in Santa Monica I spend a lot of time staring down at the shuffleboard players twenty floors down; they push their markers around on the edge of a cliff on the edge of the Pacific. Santa Monica is the most depressing town on the coast. It has no smog, it's clean, the beaches are beautiful. There's no explaining why such a goddamn brown melancholy hangs over the place.

Tom is courting his fifth wife. This one can't be more than seventeen years old. She has very small breasts, red hair, white, wide, spade-shaped cruel teeth. She's smarter than Tom. Some men are meant to live alone but Tom isn't one of them. Or if he is he hasn't found out yet.

"God-damn, Eli," he says, "why don't you do something with your life? Get married again."

2

Emily liked well-lit rooms and sex in the morning, with the television playing old comedy-show reruns. We tossed the blankets on the floor and had a hell of a good time. I miss her like crazy. Sometimes I take a walk and end up on the banks of the sad, concrete Los Angeles River and cry for us.

She lives in Lawrence, Kansas, with a professor of creative writing; he treats her better than I did. I get letters from a student of his who used to be in my classes. She says my son is doing fine and Emily looks good.

Lawrence is a little settlement of one-room cabins surrounded by a wooden stockade, set in the plains. Over it all hangs a big American paper moon.

My father and mother lived in Brooklyn with steam heat and lacy curtains. On Sunday nights he watched Ed Sullivan and she brought him bagels and cream cheese; they never talked much. My mother was always buying new carpets, appliances, curtains, mirrors, things to brighten up the apartment. My father hated them all but she never knew it; he never thought it was worth telling her. Maybe Emily and I talked too much and that was why she finally had to leave.

3

My father didn't understand about Emily's gold tooth. The day I brought her home he took me aside in the kitchen. "A gold tooth?" he said.

"What? Where? Who?" I said. The coppertone refrigerator my mother had just bought stood at my back like a monument.

"You sound like a comedian," my father said. "An Abbot and Costello. Emily is who. The second molar from the back, on the top left side. What kind of a girl has a gold tooth today? What kind of a family could she come from? Be careful, Eli."

Chester Gunn has her now, under that enormous, flat, yellow mid-continental moon—let him worry. My ex-student writes that Chester owns a green International Scout and keeps a Gatorade jar of martinis under the driver's seat. Emily sends me photographs of Kali Das and I can always pick out Chester in the background, grinning like an ape. He has a beard, and clumps of dark hair spring out of his ears. He is a wide-bellied, muscular man. When he tops my Emily she opens her mouth to moan under his weight and that yellow tooth flashes a warning.

The last time I went to Santa Monica Tom's future wife touched my thigh under the dining-room table while he was opening the wine. He went into the kitchen to slice avocadoes and she blew softly in my ear.

To live the good life in Santa Monica you have to be either a beast or a god. Tom isn't even an angel; he'd better get out before it's too late. He's losing himself. He sleeps with his secretary in motels up and down the coast when they can't get enough in the office. He writes his film scripts. He worries.

His fourth wife still loves him. Sometimes she hangs around the elevator hoping for a glimpse of Tom coming or going. Or she moons about in the park among the shuffleboard players, looking up at his windows. I've seen her leaning on the iron rail looking down at the Pacific below.

Tom believes that every man is born with an exact number of orgasms to his name. He is writing a screenplay about Cabeza de Vaca, who walked from Texas to California, another about a half-black illegitimate son of Edgar Allan Poe living in San Francisco in the days of 'forty-nine. A third is the story of a man from a distant star who has been exiled to Earth for an unnamable crime. All of them are told in Tom's slightly loony diction; he plays grab-ass with the language in ways bound to disturb and irritate the people who might buy his ideas. He worries about his work; when he turns in a script he makes a serious play for the producer's secretary so that she'll give him a running account of who in the office is reading it now, and what Tom's chances are. He's worried that all this sex is using up his assigned number too fast.

4

After our son was born Emily refused to get out of bed; I had to stay home, boil formula, change the baby, clean house, hold things together. She stayed in the bedroom with the covers pulled over her face and the television turned up extra loud. She ate alphabet soup and drank bourbon and water and ignored the kid completely. It was a son of a bitch for a few weeks and then I got the hang of it. But there was no more good sex in the morning.

Every day at ten thirty a.m. there was a rerun of Green Acres; my first memories of Kali Das are played back to me in the form of dialogue between Eddie Albert and Eva Gabor.

My sisters make similar reports on their marriages; both are still with their first husbands and both are unhappy. The husbands are solid unexceptionable men. They're in the trades and they worry about the prime rate and the labor unions. My sisters have a lot of our father in them; I predict that they're going to stick it out like he did. They also prefer not to talk, and I don't think those two solid men know how unhappy their wives are.

My father died surrounded by all of us, in the bed my grandfather bought from a man who brought it from the old country. It was an uncompromising bed: oak, black and smoky, heavy and hard as old iron. My father in his last hours was propped up against the headboard; his head hung to one side like a dead flower, and he didn't have the strength to raise it any more. To look at us at all, he had to roll his eyes up and wrinkle his forehead. True to himself he didn't say much. The two solid men sat in straight-backed chairs against the far wall; I tried to imagine them in bed with my sisters, getting some joy out of life, but I couldn't do it—the picture wouldn't come. The room smelled like camphor and stale bagels. I wanted to rush up to the bed and take my old broken father in my arms; instead I rushed down the hall to the bathroom, knelt in front of the tub and turned on the faucets. *What's the story here?* I asked myself while the cold water fell on me. I got dizzy from the noise of it in my ears, and from thinking about the solid men listening to my father's last words, in the next room but one.

5

My ex-student tells me that in Kansas when the young men can't get girls they wait until night and go after the young heifers in the fields. Lots of things apparently go on under that middle-American moonlight that can't be talked about. She offered to put me up at her place if I ever want to come out and see what it's like.

Tom took me to lunch in the Fish-Grotto; he was with one of his secretaries, a pretty girl with black hair and blue eyes.

"Did you know about Nathanael West?" I said.

"What's that?" Tom said. He looked worried.

"He was married to Eileen McKenney," I said to the girl. "The girl in *My Sister Eileen*. They died in Bakersfield because he ran a stop-sign."

"What's the matter with you?" Tom said. "For God's sake keep your voice down."

The place was full of aquariums in which strange fish moved, stately and stupid. I talked to the girl.

"Tom and I went to college together and he feels responsible for me," I said. "He wants me to do something with my life, but I don't think I will."

"You're funny," the girl said.

"For God's sake, Eli, I give up," Tom said.

"I'm a grown man," I told her. "I've got a psychiatrist and a yellow pickup truck and I can tell lies in eight languages."

"Have something to eat," Tom said.

6

It happened. Tom had his final orgasm in a motel in Laguna Beach and was forced to call off plans for his fifth marriage. It came in the middle of the night, with the motel sign flashing on and off, lighting up the wall opposite the bed, like a scene from one of the old movies Tom likes. *Where the Sidewalk Ends,* for instance. His number was up.

Emily sent Kali Das to spend Christmas with me. He is small, brown, savage and active. Like his grandfather he takes what comes without complaining. I took him to lunch at the Fish-Grotto, thinking he'd like to watch the fish. He rolled his eyes up at me while he ate, as if he was afraid I was going to steal from his plate.

My psychiatrist says it's normal for Kali Das to remind me of my father in a hundred little ways. When I tell him I'm afraid my son is going to die, he tells me it's myself I'm mourning for. Makes a certain kind of sense, if you can take seriously anything a man says who looks exactly like Shecky Greene.

If I ever went to Kansas I could dress in an inconspicuous trench coat and follow Emily and Chester Gunn around the streets of Lawrence. All the streets end at that heavy wooden wall that surrounds the town; beyond that we have the plains, crisscrossed with gullies, and the heifers and the lonesome young men. I could drive all the way out from L. A. in my yellow pickup truck, listening to Willie Nelson and not giving a damn.

A Marriage

Like jumping off a cliff, he thinks now, lying unrelaxed on his side of the bed trying to remember the old days. When he and Lee-Anne first knew each other he suffered from an enormous unreasoning desire. What it was he craved he didn't know, and he suspected right away that Lee-Anne couldn't or wouldn't give it to him, but he closed his ears to the little voices that warned him of hard times to come and married her anyhow.

Like jumping off a cliff. He gave her a T-shirt that said *once a bitch always a bitch* and she wore it gladly. Not a joke, he thinks now, lying like a log on the hard bed. He doesn't fall asleep until daylight and then he dreams he's lost in a building big as a dozen high-schools; he's wandering the halls, knowing he has to be someplace soon, but with no notion where or why.

In no time at all Lee-Anne is shaking his arm; her voice stabs his inner ear like a blade.

"Breakfast."

"All right." He comes down the hall to the bathroom still half-asleep, lost in the endless linoleum corridors of his dream; he misjudges the open door and smashes his elbow. The water gushes instantly hot from the faucet and he pulls back scalded fingers. "Son of a bitch that hurts!" he says, sucking on the burned hand. The washcloth smells like death when he holds it to his face—he knows it's only mildew but that doesn't help. His safety-razor is clogged with fine golden hairs from Lee-Anne's legs.

"Your breakfast is cold. It's your own damn fault you took so long in the bathroom."

Two fried eggs lie on his plate face-up, thick and heavy as wallpaper paste, the yolks filmed over like snake-eyes. He lays down his fork.

"What's the matter now?"

"I'm not hungry."

"What's wrong with the eggs?" She was and is a pretty girl but lately when he looks at her he sees something in her face is set against him.

"I'm not hungry."

"You're trying to humiliate me," she says.

"Stop," he says.

"You've always been a bastard. Right from the beginning. All it was, was promises. I hate your guts."

He looks at her to see if the shouting made her happy, but it didn't make much difference. Her color is high but her eyes stay impersonal. Whoever she's yelling at, it isn't him.

"And sex too," she says. "I thought you were going to be good. Ha! Another promise."

"I love you," he says like jumping off a cliff.

"Bullshit," she says. Her face is like a stone.

He picks up his plate and holds it balanced in his hand for a second, then throws it as hard as he can. It shatters on the wall above the sink. Fragments of china hail on the counter; the fried eggs slide down the red and white wallpaper.

"What do you think of that?" he says.

"You bastard. Oh you *are* a bastard. My mother gave me those plates." She kneels and begins to search for the pieces that fell all the way to the floor. She is crying.

Sometimes in the early days of the marriage the wanting, the craving had so twisted and turned him around that he didn't know what to do. He clung to her blindly whole nights at a time. He woke up cramped and fevered in the dark with his arms and legs locked around this girl he needed so badly.

He slides back his chair. She looks up from her knees. "Where are you going?" She is clutching pieces of the broken plate to her breast.

He walks into the bedroom and pulls a suitcase out of the closet. She watches him from the doorway. He takes a pair of pants and throws them in without taking them off the hanger. Shorts and rolled-up socks make a mound and he pounds it flat with his fist. He tears an armful of shirts off the pole and punches them down far enough to close the lid and click the latches.

"What are you going to do?" she says.

"I'll come back and get the rest of my things while you're at work," he says.

"I always knew you'd leave."

"I just found out myself."

"You're pretty transparent. I know more about you than you suppose."

"Probably."

"I never liked you at all," she says.

He slides the suitcase off the bed and carries it to the front door. "Good-bye," he says.

"Go ahead and leave, you son of a bitch. You parasite."

He stops. Parasite? he thinks.

"You're a contemptible parasite."

"So long," he says. "Take care of yourself."

He's gone three days in all. He comes home while she's out, throws his suitcase on the bed and goes for a walk without unpacking. He likes to walk the back streets in Van Nuys, looking over his neighbors' fences and shuffling underfoot the gaudy blooms and tropical leaves that fall from their bushes.

When he comes to the deep concrete gutter of the Los Angeles River he stops. A transplanted Midwesterner, he loves L. A., but this sad dusty canal is something else. He tries to avoid it on his walks but it winds unpredictably through his neighborhood and seems to lie in wait for him. Once he saw a dead cow lying feet-up at the bottom in three inches of water. Another time he saw a man sitting at the edge, crying.

Why did he come back? Same reason he married her—the craving. He knew better then, he knows better now, but the temptation of the leap was too much. Rapture of the heights.

That night he and Lee-Anne cling to each other in bed. "Don't ever leave me," she whispers. "Promise."

He promises. His tongue feels dusty; the passages of his nose are abandoned mines full of rotten timbers and rattlesnakes. He and Lee-Anne make love like puppies in the big bed with the air-conditioner humming an icy breeze down over their bodies. Outside it's still a hundred and two degrees—the hottest night of the year—and the smog is like sticking your head down a burning chimney. The sheets are damp; tiny wrinkles make thin lines of pain down his back. He feels that he's lost the power to move.

"I'm going to get a glass of water," he says. His mouth is full of ashes.

"So go," she says five minutes later. He hasn't moved. He wants to turn over on his side and take hold of this woman, push his head into her shoulder and make the queer procession of his thoughts come to a halt. Instead he turns the other way, slips out of bed and steps carefully past the traps laid for him by the sharp-cornered furniture. In the living-room he sits without light, holding his glass of water, watching the street-lamps bloom on top of their stainless-steel stalks.

When he comes back into the bedroom an hour later Lee-Anne is lying on her stomach with her legs slightly apart—asleep or awake, he can't tell. He climbs on top of her and slips into her slowly from the back; she says *ah* softly and he begins to stroke harder. "I love you," he whispers. He bites her neck the way he saw the roosters do it on his mother's farm in Ohio a long time back.

The quickest way across the mountains to work is through Coldwater Canyon. His old Ford is a soft-sprung machine of great power and he likes to feel it heel over in tight corners, likes to sense how the weight shifts and settles on the offside wheels and how the fat tires snatch at the pavement. He knows the pleasure he gets from this is slightly perverse and out of tune. Drivers of Hondas and Volkswagens sneer at him as he passes them, screeching and rumbling, something out of the past.

He drives it high-school style, one arm holding up the roof; the trees, some of them blazing with blue flowers, the expensive canyon houses, the lamp-posts drift by his window, tilted against the blue-gray sky. A blonde woman in a Mercedes coupe cuts into his lane without a signal and he lifts his foot to brake. Why should he be the one to leave? he thinks. Lee-Anne could go. He holds his foot poised over the brake, undecided. Why not? he thinks. If he touches the brake a little, the rich bitch will slip in ahead of him unscathed. He doesn't touch it, and the Ford kisses her bumper hard enough to give her a good jolt. He cuts the wheel and goes around her; as he passes, her startled face stares out at him through the tinted glass.

That afternoon he comes home early from work and packs

Lee-Anne's clothes for her. For himself he saves his favorite suitcase—an old heavy leather bag with brass corners—otherwise he gives her the best of the luggage. He takes her dresses out of the closet and folds them without anger. He stacks blouses, sweaters, panties, leotards, bras, handkerchiefs into the suitcases. When he's done he piles everything in the center of the living-room and sits down in the rocking chair with a drink to wait for his wife.

She stops dead at the door. The sudden shift from the glare outside to the semi-darkness of the living-room leaves her face helpless, unguarded.

"What's all this? Are you leaving again?"

"No," he says. "You are."

She looks at him over the pile of bags and boxes and gradually her face freezes into its old hardness.

"What kind of man are you?"

She disappears into the kitchen and comes back with a drink in her hand. "I wish you knew how much I hate you."

"Then it's settled."

"I never liked you at all, not even at the beginning."

"You were in love with me," he says.

"In love with you? Don't make me laugh."

"You told me I was the first man who ever made you come," he says.

"I lied."

"I wasn't the first?"

"You never made me come."

"You're lying now. What about when you screamed and moaned?"

She looks embarrassed. "I was faking."

"Wait," he says. "I need another drink." In the kitchen he opens the refrigerator and takes out the ice-cube tray. He feels calm, in control of himself. When he lets go of the freezer door it bounces back instead of latching. He slams it hard as he can; inside the refrigerator glass breaks and shelves tumble. He holds on to the edge of the sink until he feels better and can walk back into the living-room as calmly as he walked out.

"Your face is bright red," Lee-Anne tells him. "You look like you're having a heart attack."

"I never felt better," he says. He sinks into the rocking chair with a groan.

"You're going to end up alone," she says.

"In a flophouse hotel with pee-stains on my underwear," he says. But though he tries to make a joke out of it, there's cold truth in her prophecy and he knows it. For a fact he could end up alone. "I'll take the chance," he says more casually than he feels.

"You prick," she says.

"I'll help you get this stuff in your car."

A streak of sunlight comes through the window and lights up a patch of carpet at her feet, a gorgeous rusty color like an oak-leaf after the first frosts back in Ohio. For a second the color touches his heart and he wants to do or say something that will change it all to the way it could have been if everything had been different.

Lee-Anne is already carrying two suitcases to her car. Even the way her ass moves under her dress when she walks is a defiance, a denial. When her Volkswagen is loaded and sagging in the rear with the weight of all she's carrying away from him, the back wheels sadly splayed out under the load, he walks back into the house so he won't have to watch her leave. *Bitch,* he thinks, closing the door carefully.

He opens it again after a minute. Lee-Anne is standing by the car; the sun makes a long shadow starting at her feet and stretching behind her across their lawn, the neighbor's yard, finally losing itself in a cluster of palm-trees two doors down.

"I'm sorry about this," he says.

"Take care of yourself," she says.

"Had to happen."

"Nothing we could do about it," she agrees.

He tries to read her expression, but the falling sun is in her eyes and she has raised a hand to push away the orange light; the shadow crosses her face and hides her feelings.

"I guess this really is it, this time," she says. He nods.

"I'd better get going," she says.

Back inside he makes himself a peanut-butter sandwich and eats it standing up, leaning against the stove, staring across the room out the window at the neighbor's blank wall, thinking *bitch*. The peanut butter sticks to the inside of his teeth and he has another drink to wash out his mouth. The alcohol tastes pleasant and makes the back of his eyes feel warm, as if a little flame burned behind each one. He turns on the TV in time for the news. A literary agent in Malibu has discovered that the Great Pyramids of Egypt were not tombs but sophisticated machines to capture solar and spiritual energy. Above his house is a lattice-work pyramid of two-by-fours; another one encloses his bed. He has a sad face, darkly tanned, deeply wrinkled. "The earth is a space-ship," he tells the television crew.

There are grotesque accidents on the freeway: a poultry truck overturns on the San Diego and as he watches a yellow Porsche knifes through the mess, sending chickens bursting upward like ungainly angels. A fire in Santa Monica burned three children to death; oil-Arabs are moving into Beverly Hills. A man tries to fly off a cliff in Topanga Canyon; he steps off and soars hopefully for about ten feet before the fragile wings fold over his head and he falls, spread-eagled, spinning clumsily into Topanga Creek two hundred feet below.

Bitch, he thinks, watching the paramedics haul the flyer off the rocks, out of the shallow water. It's not exactly her fault, he has to admit. She's young, doesn't know that you have to give a little. Right now there's no way to live with her, but if life was to bend her a bit she might become a good person. His neighbor has a good wife; he watches them through the window sometimes; they seem to dance, to lean with each other against the tilt of the world, to sidestep the traps without trying. They're graceful as hell, the neighbors. He also suspects that they might be an exception. Marriage is an unnatural state, he thinks. He's read about those savage tribes with Men's Houses and Women's Houses, where the different sexes only come together for mating and for certain ceremonies. Maybe we've all forgotten something basic, he thinks.

He picks up the Yellow Pages and begins to make calls. Two-thirds of the way through the motels he finds her; he was smart enough to ask for her by her maiden name: Wendler. Lee-Anne Wendler—the name sent a thrill through him when he was courting her. Old-fashioned word, *courting,* he thinks. Rituals and ceremonies. Cravings. It's past midnight when he tracks her down at the Sad Tropics Motel on the coast highway, but she comes to the telephone wide-awake and calm.

"I think you should come home," he says.

He hangs up feeling both relieved and stupid. Behind him the television speaks suddenly: "What were you trying to do?"

It's the late-late news. The Topanga Canyon flier is on his hospital bed. His arms and legs are strung out on wires, cast in plaster; he is frozen in the position of the fall. His voice comes from somewhere behind the pulleys and articulated weights that hold him. The camera zooms past the wires and stops, hanging above the bandaged face; one eye is covered with a square of white gauze, the other gleams up from the bottom of a deep bruise.

"You can bet I'll make it next time," he says. "Just think what kind of a world it's going to be when everybody can fly."

Lee-Anne is going to have a baby. Happy days, he thinks; that'll bend her a little, maybe. Motherhood might settle her down. To his surprise he's right. For the first time there comes to be a certain fragility in the way she holds herself. She spends a lot of time thinking, reading, looking out the window. Her voice is softer; it no longer cuts into his ears. Some of that intolerable sureness about everything has deserted her. Changes him too. I'm going to be a father, he thinks. I'm going to raise that kid good.

Still he suspects that some of the old Lee-Anne could be lurking inside the new, waiting to come out. Like the bastard he is, he tests her.

"What do you want to name it if it's a girl?"

She stops eating to think about it. "What about Shana?"

"No relatives. Besides that's a stupid name." He watches her; the old Lee-Anne would have climbed on the horse of her anger and galloped away already. This one looks at him seriously.

"We'll call her something else," she says.

He lays down his fork and puts a hand on her stomach. "How's the baby doing anyway?"

"Fine." She gets up and stands behind his chair, puts her head on his shoulder. "I'm sure it's going to look like you."

Life is terrific, he thinks, coming down Coldwater Canyon on his way home from work. All I had to do was stick it out. He gives the old car its head and it finds a rhythm, flying left and right through the tight bends. He rolls down the driver's window and breathes in happily. Life even smells good. A baby, he thinks. Goddamn, a baby all my own. I'm going to love it.

When he gets to the red light at Ventura Boulevard he doesn't want to stop. He points the Ford up the on-ramp to the freeway. Traffic is heavy and smooth; the powerful river of cars carries him along. He turns on the FM and finds a Bach concerto. The Ventura Freeway crosses the Hollywood; twenty minutes later, still to the music of flutes and harpsichords, he swings eastward onto the Riverside. Later he rolls his window part-way up because the air is cooler, and he lights a cigarette.

He has his gasoline credit-cards in his pocket. By late morning he's in Tucson; the next day he rolls smoothly through the deserts of New Mexico: Lordsburg and Roswell and Tucumcari, listening to cowboy music, tapping his foot. The old car fairly flies.

He'll stop in El Paso, on the bitter edge of Texas. Maybe he'll call Lee-Anne. Maybe he'll turn around. Could also be he'll spread his wings like a big-assed bird and just sail on, this time. All the way back to Ohio.

Now She Sleeps

Now she sleeps. A beautiful woman who sleeps all day long in Eisenberg's bed. His fantasy bed of driftwood, knotted ropes and bits of mirror. She is nude on top of the covers, her face hidden in the pillows.

So beautiful, Eisenberg thinks, standing at the foot of the bed. Her clothes are in a heap on the floor: yellow panties, sandals, a long blue dress with darker blue flowers that remind Eisenberg of Rorschach blots. He admires her back, the indentations of the spine.

Jacob's ladder, he thinks, and wonders what that unbidden phrase has to do with anything. He admires the shape of her ass. The laugh, as always, takes him by surprise. *Quack-quack.* He cuts it off by clapping a hand hard over his mouth.

Life isn't easy for a psychiatrist who laughs like a duck and looks like a TV comic. Sad-faced. Jowly. Actually, looking ridiculous is almost a professional asset; it makes his patients feel easier about revealing their own absurdities. But that loud quacking laugh that rises from somewhere deep inside himself and bursts out without warning has him worried. At unpredictable moments some magic key in Eisenberg is touched and out comes that barnyard noise, involuntary as a hiccup, forced up and out of rational Eisenberg by . . . what? He has no idea.

Cassie sleeps. She is twenty-eight, Eisenberg forty-seven. They have no children—her choice.

He takes his hand away from his mouth, ready to slap it back again if the laugh threatens. Cassie sleeps. Eisenberg leans his forehead against the bedpost. He knows that she won't wake up before he has to leave for the clinic; he decides to skip his breakfast and watch her a little longer. Nothing to laugh about, he tells himself. Unless it's this ridiculous bed, built for him by a one-legged sculptor down from Oregon. Eisenberg met him on the beach and brought him home, a crazy-looking man who talked about making *spaces* out of *space* while he worked, bolting and pegging long pieces of driftwood together at crazy angles to make this fantasy four-poster where Eisenberg sleeps at night next to his young wife. Except when she gets up at three in the morning and wanders around in her blue dress, cooks herself little meals, sings to herself while Eisenberg twists and turns in the bed, uneasy because of too much *space*. Smoked oysters and artichoke hearts are her favorites; Eisenberg finds the open cans on the kitchen counter when he gets up in the morning. An irrational existence.

Thank God I'm not a woman, Eisenberg thinks, watching her sleep her life away.

2

Eisenberg's patients amaze him. Half the time he doesn't understand what keeps them going, but they show up at his office week after week, apparently no worse than they were the week before. How can they stand it? he asks himself, listening to their accounts of their fouled-up lives.

He sees six patients a day four days a week in the office with the dark-blue rug and the recliner chairs. Many of his patients like to stare at the ceiling while they talk to Eisenberg. He has noticed that sometimes their eyes roll as if they were seeing images up there on the white plaster. Eisenberg stays behind his desk, keeping a certain distance.

Cassie is an odd girl. She thinks the Great Quake is coming and that nothing west of the Santa Monica Mountains will survive the shake-up. He bought the house on the hill in Sherman Oaks to please her. "We'll be a little island, after the water comes," she told him. And it's turned out to be a pretty good place, though Eisenberg prefers the milder ocean climate on the other side of the ridge. Even the crazy neighbors are entertaining to Eisenberg, who likes to watch people working hard at life. This morning Lieberman woke him up hammering on the roof, putting new shingles over the hole where the tree fell. Eisenberg remembers that Cassie predicted the fall. His woman is a specialist in disasters great and small.

Norman Haas wheels in past the receptionist who holds the door open for him. He spins the wheelchair around and halts precisely in front of Eisenberg; as usual he says nothing—it's a game with him, and occasionally the psychiatrist has considered waiting him out, letting the whole session go by in silence if that's what Haas wants. Today? No, he decides.

"Did you have a good week?" Eisenberg offers.

"Did you?"

"So-so," Eisenberg says.

"I could die any day," Haas tells him. Another standard opening, but Eisenberg knows it's true. Haas can only move one arm; his chest is no bigger than a ten-year-old kid's. One bad cold could carry him away.

"We've talked about that," Eisenberg says.

"Sure. And I could still die tomorrow."

Eisenberg shrugs. "Yes."

"That's it? *Yes?* That's the best you can do?"

"Why are you so angry?"

"I don't know," Haas says. He thumbs the switch and sends the wheelchair spinning around to face away from Eisenberg. "I don't know," he says to the wall.

It's so simple, Eisenberg thinks. He waits for Haas to spin himself back into the session again.

3

Life isn't easy but it's interesting, Eisenberg thinks, driving his blue VW convertible down Ventura Boulevard to the Peacock for one drink before going home to Cassie, who will probably be asleep anyway.

A man at the bar stares at him. "Say aren't you—"

"No," Eisenberg says.

"I saw you on the TV," the man insists.

"Listen, citizen," Eisenberg says, "I just came in here for a quiet drink, so don't make trouble, all right?"

"Shecky Greene," the man says. "I'd know you anywhere. Say something funny, come on."

4

Dinnertime. Eisenberg sits across from Cassie and remembers a drive they took down to Laguna Beach in the VW. Cassie showed him a women-only bar that she and her friend Elizabeth go to sometimes. A little cave-like place set in a hill on the other side of the road from the ocean. The Eleusinia. Two old-fashioned Coca-Cola signs on either side above the entrance, shaped like bottle-caps, reminded Eisenberg of red nipples.

"What?" Cassie says. She holds a piece of trout balanced on her fork, halfway to her mouth.

"I didn't say anything."

"You said *nipples.*"

"I must have been daydreaming."

"You've been very absent-minded lately," Cassie says. She bites into the trout with obvious pleasure. "How's your steak? Did I cook it enough?"

"It's fine. Would you like some?"

"You know I don't eat meat."

"Trout is meat."

"No it isn't," she says. She lifts the backbone from the fish with the tip of her knife and sets it beside the plate.

Irrational, Eisenberg thinks. He looks at her lovingly. He needs her and he guesses that she doesn't need him. Sometimes he thinks he'd rather be married to Lieberman's wife: forty-six years old, steady, reliable, still attractive. A reasonable woman, Eisenberg thinks, though he has had glimpses of strange behavior from over there. Sheila Lieberman mothers her husband, smothers *angst* in chicken soup, drowns *weltschmerz* in sauces and homemade gravies. The sort of woman Eisenberg now and then thinks he'd rather have instead of this tall irrational blonde. A real Penelope, he thinks, envisioning Sheila Lieberman in her sewing room weaving and weaving against Lieberman's return. The new woman who lives over there now puzzles him: is she a relative? She looks a little like Lieberman, but Eisenberg knows that Lieberman's mother died a long time ago. An aunt, maybe. None of his business, Eisenberg knows, but he is passionately interested in other people's lives.

"That's why you went into psychology," Cassie says.

Eisenberg wonders how she does it. Does he make tiny unconscious movements with his lips when he's thinking?

"Angels," Cassie says. The end of a sentence Eisenberg missed.

"What?"

"I dreamed about angels last night."

"Ah," Eisenberg says.

She lays down her fork and looks him in the eye. "That's your professional bit," she says. "*Ah,* like you understand everything. Don't go professional on me," she says. "If you go professional on me I'll leave you in a minute. Remember that."

Before she moved in with Eisenberg she was a painter. Her works hang on the walls: black on black, painted with a house-painter's four-inch brush, they are furrowed, gullied, thickly textured. Black, but Eisenberg knows that if you look very closely there is always, in the center of the painting, a violent stain of red or yellow, painted over, barely perceptible. She has not painted anything since she moved in.

"Nobody could see the angels but me," Cassie says. "The air was thick with them, like dandelion puffs, and they sang a little song:

> I am dead, I am dead.
> Never never sleep in my bed.

"They sang it over and over, and everybody was terrified, even though they couldn't hear or see the angels."

"Then why were they frightened?" Eisenberg says.

"I'm not responsible for my dreams. You explain it."

"No," Eisenberg says.

She refills his wine glass; she spills a few drops on the white tablecloth where they spread slowly to make an irregular purple stain. Eisenberg stares, trying to see something in it, but it's just a stain. He lights a cigarette. Cassie stretches and yawns. "I'm sleepy now," she says.

On her way to the bedroom she stops behind his chair and touches him behind the ear. "You really are a ridiculous-looking man," she says. "But you learn fast."

Left alone, Eisenberg puffs on his cigarette; the smoke rises above his head, light as a dandelion puff. He thinks about Norman Haas with his ten-year old's chest; what kind of a life can that man live? But he's married; Eisenberg has met his wife—in his opinion a sweet girl. He finds himself humming Cassie's tune. *I am dead, I am dead / Never never sleep in my bed*.

Quack-quack-quack. Something in him wants to let the laugh fly, knowing it will get louder and louder if he doesn't stop it, begin to shake the walls, rattle the roof-beams, bring the house down. He takes himself by the throat and chokes it off.

5

On Sunday he waits for Cassie to wake up so they can eat breakfast together.

"Why don't you paint any more?" he asks her across the table.

"What would be the point?"

Eisenberg shrugs. "What's the point in anything? I like your paintings."

Cassie laughs. "No you don't. Deep down you think they must be second-rate because they were done by a woman."

"That's not true," Eisenberg says.

"You don't like women."

"I love you," Eisenberg says.

She studies him, a long measuring look past the silver candlesticks in the middle of the table. "Maybe," she says. "But that's something else altogether."

Eisenberg glances out the living-room window and sees his neighbor Lieberman walking down the street between his two women. The three of them are holding hands. "There they go," Eisenberg says.

"Lieberman's another one," Cassie says.

Women, Eisenberg thinks. He wouldn't be surprised to see those two begin to pull on Lieberman's arms until they tore him apart in a frenzy. The thought, like the laugh, comes from someplace dark. *Pater*, he thinks. *Pattern. A shape*.

"I see people every day who don't have any order in their

lives," he says to Cassie. "It's not pretty." Actually, he thinks, that's not completely true. They have order, but it's the wrong kind.

"Doodly-shit," Cassie says.

The words hurt Eisenberg.

"Don't pout," Cassie says. She yawns. "I'm going out with Elizabeth tonight. You'll have to get your own dinner."

"When will you be home?"

"Don't push me," Cassie says.

"Do you think I really look like Shecky Greene?" Eisenberg asks her.

She thinks about it for a second. "Just about exactly," she says. "You could be twins."

Just about exactly, Eisenberg thinks. Only a woman would use words with such disregard for what they mean. Left alone they would destroy the language. He wonders what she does with Elizabeth when they go out together. Sometimes Cassie doesn't come home until early morning. He wakes up when she slides into the fantasy bed beside him, where she immediately goes to sleep. Four o'clock, five o'clock. He gets up and makes himself coffee and reads professional journals in the living-room until it's time for him to go to the clinic. Or else he lies beside his wife, wide-awake, wondering.

Eisenberg is impressed with the power of women to have strong emotions, and also to conceal them so well. To let themselves go out of control, and to hold themselves in tight when it's to their advantage. He can't do either one very well. Cassie, on the other hand, would kill him—in the right circumstances—or else stand and laugh at him, controlling herself. *Don't push me,* is her advice. Good advice, Eisenberg knows. Sometimes he thinks that Cassie cannot really believe that anyone beside herself has any objective existence; other times, watching her, he's sure she knows, but that she doesn't care.

What would it be like to be a woman? he asks himself. What would it be like to fly? What is man that I should be mindful of him? Could I be a woman and still be Eisenberg? From his father, a motorman on the New York subway, Eisenberg inherited a railroad watch that he sometimes swings on its silver chain to hypnotize patients, and a handful of religious convictions which float up to the surface of his mind when he neither needs nor wants them. Man and woman created He them. He didn't know what He was doing, Eisenberg thinks. He watches Lieberman come back up the street, still held between his two loving women, still in one piece. Eisenberg parts the curtains slightly for a better look. Lieberman is smiling. *Idiot,* Eisenberg thinks. *Blind man. Fool.*

6

Norman Haas misses a month of appointments without calling. When he comes again Eisenberg sees that they've put a plastic tube in the hollow of his neck.

"I died," Haas says.

Show concern, Eisenberg tells himself. He feels it, but he's not certain he can show it. "You died? Really died?"

"Once at home and then three more times in the hospital. Ellie has to plug me into a respirator at night. What do you think of that?" The tube is white plastic, with a blue center like a breath-mint. Eisenberg realizes that the blue dot is a plug to close the tube so that Norman can breathe normally and talk when he's not on the respirator, but the image of the breath-mint keeps recurring. Suddenly the duck-laugh rattles his back teeth; under cover of his desk he gives himself a vicious punch in the diaphragm to make it stop.

Haas stares at him, but before Eisenberg can apologize he begins to laugh too. Eisenberg can see that it hurts him; the tube moves in and out and the psychiatrist is afraid that something will pop, the blue plug will fly out under the strain and Norman will start whistling horribly through the open hole.

Haas gasps and finally stops. "You remember what you told me once? You said that all my jokes end in death. I told Ellie and she said I should switch therapists."

Ellie is his wife; she bathes Norman, helps him from bed to wheelchair and back again, drives him around Los Angeles in the VW bus. Instead of a back seat it has clamps bolted to the floor to hold the wheelchair steady while she maneuvers. Another Penelope there, Eisenberg thinks. But what is she underneath? What are any of them really? He has a great itch to find out. But how can he?

"I'm a lot better now," Haas says. "I don't even really need the respirator, except that Ellie is afraid I might just forget to keep breathing some night. She loves me. I don't know what she'll do when I'm gone."

"What do you think she'll do?" Eisenberg says, sliding them into another session.

7

Mysteries, Eisenberg thinks. Five o'clock in the morning and he is lying next to Cassie. She sleeps with unnatural quiet; he has to lay a hand on her back to feel her breathe and be sure she's not dead. He thinks of all the mysterious places where women go to be alone with each other. The health spas, the women's rooms in restaurants and night clubs, the women-only bars like the one in Laguna Beach. What do they do there, Eisenberg wonders.

He remembers his mother and her three sisters whispering in the kitchen and the way they suddenly shut up when his father walked in. His father's blustering and joking to cover up his embarrassment. His fear as well, Eisenberg now thinks. Eisenberg remembers the day he walked into the wrong door in the shopping mall in Westwood and looked up from his preoccupation to find himself in a damp cave full of the buzzing of hair-dryers and the metallic smell of permanents and dyes. Two hefty black women in white gowns drove him out with flapping towels and cries of horror. Lying in his own bed here a year later Eisenberg still blushes.

Caught in the ropes of this bed dreamed up by the one-legged madman from Oregon are little fragments of mirror that throw Eisenberg back at himself in bits and pieces: a nose, an eye, the back of his head, a foot. It's an hour or more before dawn and he has only the dim off-color light of the street-lamps outside to see himself by. What do women do when they're alone together?

Eisenberg would give anything to know. He can't ask Cassie, asleep beside him. They won't tell.

8

Norman Haas is dead. Eisenberg has just come back from witnessing the end. Cassie is gone again with Elizabeth; the note carelessly Scotch-taped to the corner of one of her paintings —where, however, it was bound to catch his eye—tells him not to wait up.

Haas sent telegrams to all the women who had been important in his life, asking them to come be with him at the end. A living wake. Eisenberg spent the afternoon sitting next to Norman's bed among strangers. Beyond his strictly professional obligation, he told himself, but what the hell, it wasn't something he could refuse a dying man. Ellie walked among them with cookies and cups of tea; she plugged and unplugged Norman from the respirator so he could talk. Eisenberg was wedged between Norman's mother and Norman's high-school sweetheart, flown in from Moline, Illinois. The mother sat stone-faced while Haas sank slowly. Toward the end of the afternoon he stopped talking, stayed on the respirator, turned darker and darker in the face, finally died, though his ten-year-old's chest continued to pump up and down until Ellie switched off the machine. The middle-aged sweetheart sobbed into a blue bandanna. An unidentified woman in the corner, sitting apart from the others, scratched at her face, leaving long red welts. A mistress? Eisenberg didn't know.

Possibly, Eisenberg thinks, standing in front of Cassie's painting, the strangest afternoon of his life. He feels out of place in the world and he has to read Cassie's note three times before he gets the message.

He sits in the living-room eating a can of Cassie's sardines, leaning forward so he won't drip oil on himself. When the doorbell rings he jumps up and almost spills everything.

Lieberman's new woman considers him gravely, standing in the doorway. Up close she doesn't look as much like Lieberman as he had thought.

"Excuse me," she says.

"Come in." He takes a step back and gestures with the hand that still holds the sardine-can. Oil drips on his clothes. "Damn," he says. "Come in, come in." He hears the hunger for company in his own voice. It's that weird afternoon, he tells himself. All those women crying. Poor Norman dead.

Lieberman's woman sits down beside him on the couch. "He's better off," she says. "What kind of life could he have had?"

"Like the rest of us," Eisenberg says.

"Do you believe in life after death?"

"That's silliness. Like astrology or astral travel. Or devils." As he denies these things which he has not believed in since he was twelve years old, he feels them becoming true. "Silliness for people who can't face life like it is," he says.

"You really believe that?"

"I'm glad I'm not a woman," Eisenberg says. "Women need mysteries and hocus-pocus or they can't live." He's never thought of it just like this before but now he sees with magical clarity; the words roll off his tongue before he can think them, they bubble out of him. *Angelical,* he thinks, though his father taught him not to believe in angels. However it seems the only word for what is happening to him. He feels possessed, inspired.

"Life is life," Eisenberg says. The woman nods, encouraging him to go on. She reaches out and lays a hand on his hand; the dry feathery contact makes him shiver. "Yes," he says. "That's exactly what it is. No mysteries." The hand stays there on his, light as . . . dandelion seed is the word that pops into his head. He remembers Cassie's dream.

After the woman leaves, Eisenberg wanders into the bedroom to change his clothes. He undresses slowly. The mirror shows him a body still lean, unwrinkled, healthy. Eisenberg jogs three times a week around the golf course in Reseda. Not because he likes it, or because it makes him healthy, but because while he's running he feels he just might live forever. He turns slowly, watching himself in the full-length glass. Not bad, he says out loud. He feels suddenly dizzy, full of possibilities he doesn't understand and is terrified to explore. Strange goddamn world, he thinks. With strange goddamn people in it.

He walks into the closet and comes back carrying a bundle. He shakes it out in front of the mirror: Cassie's blue dress, the yellow panties, a long scarf, her sandals.

I can't, he thinks.

But once in the blue dress, he feels strangely free, unbound by his ideas. He twirls slowly in front of the glass. Now the scarf, he tells himself. He ties it under his chin, peasant-style. Now the sandals.

No longer Eisenberg, he takes a few soft steps away from the mirror, tilts his head to one side, considers the reflected figure. Nice shade of blue, he thinks.

9

Eisenberg parks the VW across the street from the Eleusinia. He takes out the little mirror from Cassie's purse and looks at himself. Rouge, lip-gloss and eyeshadow have changed his face, erased the jowls and raised the cheekbones. He wipes a speck of red from his front tooth.

Nobody challenges him when he walks through the door under the twin Coca-Cola signs. Inside it is as dark as he had dreamed it would be; it smells musky and sweet, like his mother's root-cellar in summer. Inside his dress Eisenberg feels naked, open to assault. The yellow panties rub him in unaccustomed places; the sandals bind his feet and make his walking clumsy—he couldn't run to save his life. He picks a table near the back wall. No Cassie here tonight, unless that tall woman on the other side of the room is his wife; false eyelashes make it hard for Eisenberg to see clearly without opening his eyes unnaturally wide.

The room is full of dappled motion, rich colors swirling in the dark: dresses of cerise and puce, lavender and robin's egg blue. A red-headed waitress appears at his table.

"What'll it be, honey?"

"Bourbon," Eisenberg says. His natural voice is high for a man; it will pass.

"Straight up?" the waitress says. She clings to the edge of the table with fingernails the color of blood.

"What?"

"Straight up, with water, how do you want it? Don't take all night, honey, we're busy."

"On the rocks," he says. "I'm sorry."

"Sure," she says. "Just relax, honey, we're all friends here. Didn't mean to snap at you."

Excited, Eisenberg peers around the room after she walks away, trying to see everything. Is that the sweetheart from Moline laughing to herself over there in the corner? Suddenly nervous, he reaches up to his scarf to make sure it's still in place. Surely that iron-faced woman two tables away is one of his old patients. Martha Teller—the one whose son lived with a bear in Beverly Hills. Eisenberg turns his head away, frightened that she'll recognize him. Hardest woman he ever met. Capable of anything, he remembers, as long as she thinks she is doing it out of love or human charity. But he can't keep his head turned to the wall all night—he has to see. Isn't that why he came?

"Here's your drink, honey."

Startled, Eisenberg jumps guiltily.

"Say you are nervous, aren't you? What's the matter? Boyfriend dump you? Troubles at home? You came to the right place to get away from it."

Eisenberg shakes his head. He's suddenly convinced that his voice would give him away. Some of the women are dancing together, and he peers at them through the smoke. They seem to be having a good time. Their faces are quiet, free of the tension Eisenberg sees in the women he meets out in the world.

Here comes Cassie now; he can't understand how he missed her before. She is in the arms of a short dark woman who wears dangling earrings of silver and jade. This might be Elizabeth; Eisenberg has never met her. Cassie's head rests on her shoulder; she spins right past Eisenberg's table and he stares into his wife's face, soft and somehow naked. The woman is embracing Cassie tightly, possessively. The earrings brush against Cassie's cheek as she bends and glides and dips to the music.

She never looked like that for me, jealous Eisenberg thinks. The music steps up its tempo; the women are whirling and jumping now. Long hair flames in the spotlights, shakes out cascades of color that dazzle Eisenberg, who is turning and twisting his head, trying to look everywhere at once.

Dear God, he whispers. Louder, faster. Like spooked horses the women fly apart, leap and arch their backs in the dance. Cassie appears for a moment in front of him; her eyes are wild, her mouth open, her arms outstretched; her feet leave the floor in impossible bounds.

She comes back to dance in front of Eisenberg; he wants to turn away but can't. "Come on," she cries to him. "Come on!" She reaches out for him; her hand brushes against the scarf and it falls.

"Man!" somebody screams. "A man!"

A hand reaches for the front of his dress; he pulls away, but the wall is at his back; the fingers twist his nipples cruelly. The dancers close in and yank him out of his chair. "Cassie!" he cries out. Martha Teller leans over him. "Animal," she hisses, and tears out a handful of hair.

From the floor Eisenberg stares up at the ring of frenzied faces. *Dear God*, he thinks. *Master of the Universe*. Fingernails slash at his eyes, rake across his cheeks, drawing blood. One sandal is dragged off.

The blue dress is ripped away by a dozen hands, revealing Eisenberg in yellow panties. He tries to cover himself but his arms are pinned, stretched out, pulled until he feels the joints crack. The sweetheart from Moline spits in his face. He senses fingers groping at his crotch, tearing the yellow silk, touching flesh.

Quack-quack-quack. The laugh explodes out of his mouth like a huge shout. He lets it come. He flaps on the floor like a great wounded bird. Above him the room begins to shake and shiver; the ceiling cracks. Eisenberg laughs and laughs.

My Life Is a Screenplay

EXT. DAY: THE SAN DIEGO FREEWAY NEAR THE
SANTA MONICA INTERCHANGE. FROM ABOVE.

The multiple cloverleaf, a function of the crossing of freeways, is revealed from above as a thing of beauty. The cars move slowly, carried by a powerful stream whose invisible water is greed, habit, the fear of not-being-a-man-in-the-world. To the far right, a golden speck on a white steeple is the Angel Moroni standing on one foot on top of the Temple, getting ready to blow his horn. We hear the frantic flap-flap of the helicopter which holds us poised above everyday-life—the wing-beats of a terrible mechanical angel.

INT. CAR, DAY: MYSELF AND BUDDY BROWN
IN MY YELLOW PORSCHE

We are moving by fits and starts, caught by the traffic: clutch-brake-clutch-accelerator-clutch-brake. The plugs are oiling up on this machine which can do a hundred and thirty miles an hour on the flat and drift through high-speed bends with saintly precision.

"I was in all the way," Buddy says. "Seventy-five hundred against a hundred thousand and points if they made the film. George loved the idea."

"They should have given you ten against a hundred," I say.

"My agent didn't push." Buddy shrugs as if he doesn't care.

I gun the Porsche to shut off a Mercedes trying to squeeze ahead of me.

"He said we'd make it up in the package."

"Agents," I say.

"Schmucks," Buddy says.

"And what happened?" I already know but he needs to tell it to me again this morning; I just want him to get done before we turn off on the Santa Monica, so we can talk a little about today's business. Buddy is forty years old this year, like me; I understand something about his needs.

"Forget it," he says. "Let's talk about *Billy Budd.*"

EXT. DAY: THE PORSCHE CLIMBING COLDWATER CANYON

I am alone at the wheel. My face shows anxiety, exasperation, foreknowledge of bad things.

STREET SIGN: WONDERLAND DRIVE

The street is empty, silent. The yellow Porsche comes nosing cautiously around the corner.

EXT. HOUSE: SAME STREET

Resawn cedar planks, glass, redwood decks. A BMW is parked at the curb.

MY POV

I go up the driveway. The garage door is open; the Porsche slides in. I shut it off; it backfires and dies. I get out and close the garage door.

INT. BEDROOM

I am in bed with a woman; we are clearly naked under a green silk sheet. Neither of us looks happy to be there. The headboard is a giant photo blow-up of Shirley Temple; her baby teeth are as big as soup-plates. Above the bed is a light-fixture from a pool-hall—long, rectangular, with several bulbs. The theme is carried out by wires stretched from bedpost to bedpost, with sliding wooden counters.

"Why do you come to see me?" she says.

"Everybody has needs," I say.

"Look at this place," she says. "What kind of person would want a bedroom like a pool-hall?"

"I don't want to talk about Buddy," I say.

"You love him," she says.

The man who is me doesn't answer.

"So what are you doing in bed with his wife?" she says.

EXT. DAY: BUDDY AND I ARE WALKING ALONG A STREET IN VENICE

"I've got nothing against Alonzo," Buddy says. "He wants to direct a picture now, why not? What's a director? I'm ready to go, George is ready to go, that bastard Alonzo shakes my hand and tells me he loves my story. It's like Brotherhood Week."

The sky is pale blue; the thinnest fog you can imagine is floating in off the ocean.

"I don't hear anything for a month," Buddy says. "Then they call me in and the first thing I see in George's office is Alonzo looking sorrowful and uneasy, like Don Quixote with a hard-on. 'I can't shoot this script,' he says."

We are walking by a playground; kids are shooting a dirty red white and blue American Association basketball through a hoop strung with chains.

"Alonzo has this young friend who's a writer," Buddy says.

"Ah," I say.

"The kid has a new script which even George can see after reading two pages is a piece of garbage. His idea of dialogue sounds like *Tom Swift and his Electric Flying Machine*. Terrible."

"You have to have an ear," I say.

"He went to Yale Drama School," Buddy says. "They don't know from ears at Yale."

"So why didn't they go back to your script?"

"George couldn't offend Alonzo; they've got him signed up to do three pictures. They'll just keep the kid doing rewrites until he gets tired."

"At five thousand a shot?"

"Ten," Buddy says.

"You have to love this town," I say.

Buddy shrugs. "What the hell—the kid can use the experience and it's deductible, so why should George give a damn?"

"Don't you feel you got screwed?"

"Getting screwed builds character; who learns from winning? I can use the experience too."

We walk away down the street. On the roof of one of the buildings is a billboard that once showed an old cowboy smoking a cigarette; the wind has torn away everything but his hat. At the bottom of the billboard, in red letters: YOU HAVE TO LOVE THIS MAN.

INT. DAY: A REAL-ESTATE OFFICE IN SAN CLEMENTE

Millicent is at her desk, surrounded by vigorous plants.

"What is it?" she says. "What are you doing here?"

"Relax, angel," I say. "I'm just playing it by ear. I drove down figuring that when I saw you it would come to me."

"What would come to you?"

"So I figured wrong," I say.

She looks at me closely. I know the look. "You've changed," she says. "You've become a little crazy lately. If I were you I'd watch it. Are you still seeing Richard?"

"Richard and Max are doing a new save-yourself paperback together this year. I got tired of him trying out his last chapter on the group every week."

She leans forward over her desk. "You ought to take better care of yourself," she says with phony compassion. "You look tired."

"Buddy and Ellen were asking about you," I say to get her off that subject.

"I'm doing fine," she says.

INT. NIGHT: BUDDY'S HOUSE, A PARTY

Buddy is propped up on a sofa; his face has the peculiar expression of extreme concentration worn by someone who is nine-tenths drunk and feels that the world, no longer sharply separated from himself, will float off into the unnameable void if he doesn't watch it closely.

"I'm doing fine," he says slowly. "Don't worry about me."

At two o'clock in the morning the old party has wound down and a new one, made up of people who begin to function after midnight, is taking shape.

The bartender is a beautiful young man whose head, like that of many young actors, is subtly too large for his body. Not so much the head, actually—the face. It clicks digitally from one emotion to the next. He is talking to an extraordinary blonde in a white evening gown.

"I don't have to do this." He makes a gesture that includes Buddy's liquor, Buddy's guests, and Buddy himself, who is still concentrating on holding the world in place.

"It's research. You know—how people act. To be an actor you have to know everything about people. You have to be a psychologist. I could tell you what any person here is going to do before they do it."

I focus on the blonde. Dressed in boy's clothes she could play Billy Budd to break anybody's heart if we ever make the movie. Uncanny innocence. Born fully formed from an egg ten minutes ago. She points to me.

"Tell me what he's going to do."

I could write a sonnet sequence on the occasion of the curve of her lower lip, if I could write sonnets. In the last scene we could not hang her; the sight of the uncaring, stiff rope knotted around her neck would be more already than the audience could stand.

"Don't strain yourself," I tell the bartender. "What I'm going to do is order a drink."

His face clicks through two or three expressions as he takes in my age, my expensive haircut, the denim leisure suit from Rodeo Drive, and decides I might be somebody. It settles on respectful attention with a touch of arrogance.

The body underneath the face signals it would like to punch me in the mouth for interfering with his pursuit of this extraordinary blonde. The contrast reminds me of the painted flats through which you could stick your head and be photographed with the body of Charles Atlas or Popeye the Sailor at Coney Island thirty years ago.

"What I'm going to do," I tell the blonde, "is have one for the road and go home. Leave your phone number with Buddy; we might have something interesting for you. Bushmill's," I tell the kid. "No ice, no water."

EXT. SAME NIGHT: BUDDY'S FRONT DOOR

I step out, turn back to wave at somebody still inside.

MY POV

I start to get into the Porsche, parked down the street, and find Buddy's wife sitting inside.

"Get in," she says.

"Where are we going?"

"I'm hungry. Let's go find an all-night deli. Or Tex-Mex. I like that too. Come on, let's roll."

The Porsche goes slowly down the street, flashing lemon-yellow, lemon-yellow when it passes under the sodium lights.

"Do you know how long it is since I've thought about Coney Island?" I say. "We never outgrow what we did when we were kids. I'm stuck in the nineteen-forties until I die."

"Don't talk about dying," she says.

"All right."

"Who was the little girl with the tits?"

"That's another thing I can't get used to," I say. "All this free and easy sex."

"You know what the girls call it now?" she says. "Taking a shower."

INT. BAYOU BOB'S BARBECUE: SAME NIGHT

"Let's run away," she says. "Let's go anyplace. El Paso."

"I've been to El Paso," I say. "It isn't worth the drive. Eat up and I'll take you home."

"To Buddy," she says. "That's Coney Island talking."

"You like me because I'm old-fashioned," I say.

"How's Millie?"

"Terrific. She's selling real-estate now. Last month she met Nixon. Isn't the world crazy?"

"It's going to hell," she says.

INT. DAY: DECONCINI'S OFFICE

Buddy and I are sitting on half of his sofa, leaving room for his Irish setter, who lies with his muzzle between his legs, staring at the Oriental rug.

"What do you think of my office-girl?" DeConcini says.

"Great tits," Buddy says automatically.

"Her husband's a cop," DeConcini says. "She works two nights a week as a decoy hooker for the L.A.P.D. She puts on hotpants and a transparent blouse and walks up and down the Strip while the Vice Squad watches her.

The dog has gone to sleep; he snores; from time to time his front paws twitch sharply.

"Well I think you've got a hell of a story there, myself," DeConcini says. "It's definitely a classic. Only my experience is that sea-stories are poison." He shrugs. "People won't go see them. What if we brought it up to date and set it in, say, peace-time Germany with the American troops. Then we could get the drug problem—that's still getting a lot of play in the papers. I mean there's no reason why this Starry Vere couldn't be an *Army* captain, is there?"

"We'll need some money up front for the rewrite," Buddy says.

"Wait a minute—" I sit up and the dog lifts his head half an inch to stare at me with sad eyes.

"You don't like it?" DeConcini says.

"He loves it," Buddy assures him.

INT. BAR: SAME AFTERNOON

Buddy and I are sitting across from each other in a booth. The table is full of empty glasses, which he has refused to let the waitress clear.

"Why don't you and I get out of this business?" he says.

The waitress, who has great tits, comes bringing two more beers and he shoves all the loose coins and bills on the table in her direction.

"Keep it all, little girl," he says. A quarter rolls on the floor and he picks it up and puts it in her hand.

"Be an angel," he says. "Bring me a little something to eat. An egg. A stick of meat. Whatever you've got."

"Millie said to say hello," I say.

"Millicent is one of the two toughest broads I ever met," Buddy says. "She'll make out better than you. How long's it been since you two split?"

"Two years."

"Wives," he says. "You can't ever tell about wives. Why'd she up and leave you like that? Was she screwing around with somebody else?"

"I left *her,*" I say.

He doesn't hear me. "You can't ever tell," he says again. "Ellen, for instance. She's fucking somebody—I know that."

The waitress comes back with a boiled egg and a pepperoni stick wrapped in cellophane.

"Pay her," Buddy says. He rolls the egg on the tabletop to crack the shell. "But I don't know why," he says. "That's the part which is a mystery to me."

He bites into the egg and stares across the table at me. "You have any idea?"

INT. BEDROOM: DAY

The green sheets have been replaced with chalky blue. Afternoon light comes in lemon-colored slices through a wooden Venetian blind.

"Did you remember to put the garage door down?" she says.

"Yeah."

"Want to take a shower?"

"No," I say. "Let's talk."

She blows blue smoke at the wooden beads on their taut wire.

"What I'd like to know is why me?" she says. "I'm complicated and I'm a pain in the neck and I'm not such a good lay. There are so many little girls around this town that would love to go to bed with you."

"I wouldn't love to go to bed with them," I say. After a minute I say "Do you suppose Buddy knows?"

"*I* haven't told him. Has he ever said anything to you?"

"No."

She coughs. "He wouldn't, anyway. Not straight out. He's subtle. Anyway he loves you too; that makes it complicated."

"Let's not talk about Buddy, OK?"

"You started it."

"Let's not."

"Answer my question, then. Why me? Why not that little blonde from the party, for instance?"

"Particular needs," I say.

"Oh God!" she says. "Get me another cigarette. No, not one of yours; I hate filters. The Gauloises—they're on top of the dresser."

MY POV

I look out through the Venetian blind and see strips of Wonderland Drive. A bunch of kids dressed like angels come around the corner. They wear bedsheets for robes, have cardboard wings painted with curlicues of gold to signify feathers, and haloes made of coat-hanger wire.

"Close the blinds," she says. "That goddamn sunlight all the time depresses me. Go on, close them. Why the hell doesn't it rain here anymore?"

"If it did you'd be depressed because it was raining."

"Are you trying to tell me I'm neurotic?" she says.

"Like everybody."

"I was happy when I was a kid," she says.

"I wasn't."

"I don't know why I was," she says. "We lived in Bakersfield and we were poor. I was scrawny and the boys didn't like me. My daddy didn't have any money at all. Why was I happy?"

"I don't know."

"I was, though," she says.

"All right," I say. "I believe you."

"We could be happy now. We could do it if we really tried."

"That's a laugh," I say.

INT. DAY: ALICE'S RESTAURANT ON THE MALIBU PIER

Buddy is laughing.

Outside the pelicans are falling one by one, headfirst into the water like feathery bombs, diving for fish. Old men with closed faces like fists are dangling lines into the sea. Tourists are taking pictures of each other.

Buddy is laughing.

"You think it's a funny idea?" I say.

"I love it," he says. "Who'd play Starry Vere?"

"Stacy Keach."

"Perfect," Buddy says.

"A comic hanging, right?"

"Naturally. What about Billy Budd?"

The waitress stands at his elbow with our onion soup. He ignores her.

"Buddy Hackett," I say. "A fat Billy Budd. What about Claggart?"

He accepts the two soups, passes me one. "Keenan Wynn?"

I shake my head. "No good."

"OK," he says. "Who?"

"Wait a minute." I blow on my soup, look at the pelicans for a clue. "Jack Elam."

"Ah," Buddy says. "Perfect." He holds up a finger to call the waitress back. "Little girl, how about bringing us another drink—I think we're inspired."

Outside the pelicans soar like angels. The tourists are afraid and huddle together, faces turned to the sky. It's the end of the world.